A PU... ...VERSE

This anthology is intended simply to give pleasure, and it is hoped that every boy or girl who browses among its pages will find something to enjoy.

It ranges from nursery rhymes and nonsense poems to verses whose meaning has to be thought about: but whether the poems are simple or more difficult, they have been chosen partly for that beauty of rhythm and language which makes lines linger in the mind after the book that contains them has been put aside.

A PUFFIN BOOK OF

VERSE

COMPILED BY ELEANOR GRAHAM

With decorations by Claudia Freedman

PENGUIN BOOKS

Penguin Books Ltd, Harmondsworth, Middlesex, England
Penguin Books Inc., 7110 Ambassador Road, Baltimore, Maryland 21207, U.S.A.
Penguin Books Australia Ltd, Ringwood, Victoria, Australia

—

First published 1953
Reprinted 1955, 1957 1959, 1960, 1963, 1964, 1965, 1967, 1968, 1969, 1970

—

This selection copyright © Eleanor Graham, 1953

—

Made and printed in Great Britain
by Hunt Barnard Printing Ltd, Aylesbury
Set in Monotype Bembo

Contents

CONTENTS

6. MAGIC AND ROMANCE

CONTENTS

CONTENTS

Foreword

I HAVE had a simple standard in compiling this anthology for children, namely to find verses which sing in the ear and catch in the mind. Some are mere doggerel, others the sublime expression of great adult minds; yet it appears to me that each has some clear appeal to the simplicity of youth.

An anthology is only made by gleaning other men's thoughts, and I wish to acknowledge the debt with gratitude and to thank all those, whether living or dead, who have contributed to this volume.

Especially I should like to thank the late Anna Wickham for the passionate sincerity of her poem 'Domestic Economy'; W. H. Ogilvie for lending the romantic beauty of his ballad, 'The Raiders'; Naomi Mitchison for her lines on 'Spring', which first appeared in *Time and Tide;* and Barbara Euphan Todd for her verses 'Sing a Song of Honey', and 'The Calendar' (reproduced by permission of the proprietors of *Punch*).

I have also to thank the following for permission to reprint copyright matter: the proprietors of *Country Life* for the poem by G. James; the author and Duckworth & Co. Ltd, for the poem 'Sevens' by Eleanor Farjeon; the author and Methuen and Co. Ltd, for the poem by C. Fox Smith; Helen Thomas and Faber & Faber Ltd, for the poem by Edward Thomas; Burns Oates and Washbourne Ltd, and the Newman Press for the poem by Francis Thompson; Sidgwick and Jackson Ltd, and the author's representatives for W. J. Turner's 'Romance', reprinted from his *Poems*.

The poems by Constance Holme, Irene McLeod, Padraic Colum, and Dr E. V. Rieu are included by permission of the authors.

Robert Bridges' 'Spring Goeth all in White' is reprinted from *The Shorter Poems of Robert Bridges* (Clarendon Press, Oxford), by permission of Mrs Bridges and the publishers; Elizabeth Coatsworth's 'The Mouse' from *Compass Rose*, by Elizabeth Coatsworth, copyright 1929 by Coward-McCann, Inc., by permission of the author; Walter de la Mare's 'Some One Came Knocking', 'The

Song of the Mad Prince', and 'Jim Jay' from *Collected Poems*, by
Walter de la Mare (Faber & Faber Ltd), copyright U.S.A. 1920,
by Henry Holt and Company Inc., copyright 1948 by Walter de
la Mare, by permission of the author and publishers; and Thomas
Hardy's 'Weathers' from *The Collected Poems of Thomas Hardy*, by
permission of the Trustees of the Hardy Estate and Macmillan and
Co., and from *Collected Poems*, copyright 1925 by the Macmillan
Company, U.S.A., with their permission.

Acknowledgements are also due to Eleanor Farjeon for per-
mission to include her poem 'Christmas Carol: God Bless your
House this Holy Night', from *Sing for your Supper*, published in
England by Michael Joseph and in the U.S.A. by J. B. Lippincott
Co.; to the author, Duckworth & Co., Ltd, and Alfred A. Knopf
for Hilaire Belloc's 'Charles Augustus Fortescue' and 'Matilda –
Who Told Lies', and to George Allen & Unwin for the same
author's 'The End of the Road' from *The Path to Rome;* to the
Society of Authors as the Literary Representative of Miss Rose
Fyleman for her 'Alms in Autumn' from *The Fairy Queen*, by Rose
Fyleman, copyright 1923 by Doubleday and Company, Inc.; and
to Sidgwick and Jackson Ltd for John Drinkwater's 'Birthright', reprinted by permission of the author's Estate, from *Collected Poems*,
copyright 1919 by John Drinkwater. A. E. Housman's 'Loveliest
of Trees' is reprinted from *A Shropshire Lad* by permission of Henry
Holt and Company Inc., U.S.A., the Society of Authors as the
Literary Representatives of the Trustees of the Estate of the late
A. E. Housman, and Jonathan Cape Ltd, publishers of his *Collected Poems;* and James Joyce's 'Chamber Music', copyright 1918
by B. W. Huebsch, 1946 by Nora Joyce, is reprinted by permission
of the Viking Press, Inc., New York, Jonathan Cape Ltd, and the
Trustees of the James Joyce Estate.

E. G.

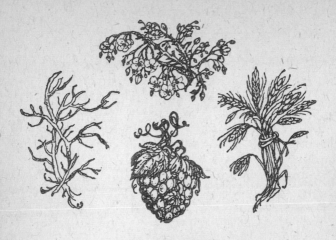

1 · THE SEASONS

—

The Months of the Year

SARA COLERIDGE

January brings the snow;
Makes the toes and fingers glow.

February brings the rain,
Thaws the frozen ponds again.

March brings breezes loud and shrill,
Stirs the dancing daffodil.

April brings the primrose sweet,
Scatters daisies at our feet.

May brings flocks of pretty lambs,
Skipping by their fleecy dams.

June brings tulips, lilies, roses;
Fills the children's hands with posies.

Hot July brings cooling showers,
Strawberries and gilly-flowers.

August brings the sheaves of corn,
Then the Harvest home is borne.

Warm September brings the fruit,
Sportsmen then begin to shoot.

Fresh October brings the pheasant;
Then to gather nuts is pleasant.

Dull November brings the blast,
Then the leaves are falling fast.

Chill December brings the sleet,
Blazing fire and Christmas treat.

The Cuckoo

ANONYMOUS

Cuckoo, Cuckoo,
What do you do?

In April
I open my bill.

In May
I sing night and day.

In June
I change my tune.

In July
Away I fly.

In August,
Go I must.

Spring Goeth all in White

ROBERT BRIDGES

Spring goeth all in white,
Crowned with milk-white may:
In fleecy flocks of light
O'er heaven the white clouds stray:

White butterflies in the air;
White daisies prank the ground:
The cherry and hoary pear
Scatter their snow around.

I Bended unto Me

T. E. BROWN

I bended unto me a bough of may,
That I might see and smell:
It bore it in a sort of way,
It bore it very well.
But when I let it backward sway,
Then it were hard to tell
With what a toss, with what a swing,
The dainty thing
Resumed its proper level,
And sent me to the devil.
I know it did – you doubt it?
I turned, and saw them whispering about it.

Spring

NAOMI MITCHISON

Behind the leaves and the rain
The cuckoo shouts again.
Winter was death and pain
But the wallflower's sweet again.
The body relaxes strain,
The blood flows easy again.
Malcolm and Donalbain,
The young sons of the slain,
Leap to their feet again.
Beeches and oak again,
Foxes and hares again,
The thing I could not explain
Has all come steady and plain,
And the clock stops in my brain.

Our Trees in Spring

E. NESBIT

The silver birch is a dainty lady,
    She wears a satin gown;
The elm tree makes the old churchyard shady,
    She will not live in town.

The English Oak is a sturdy fellow,
    He gets his green coat late;
The willow is smart in a suit of yellow,
    While brown the beech trees wait.

Such a gay green gown God gave the larches –
    As green as He is good!
The hazels hold up their arms for arches,
    When Spring rides through the wood.

The chestnut's proud, and the lilac's pretty,
    The poplar's gentle and tall,
But the plane tree's kind to the poor dull city,
    I love him best of all.

The Borrowed Days

ANONYMOUS

March said to Aperill,
'I see three hoggies on a hill,
And if you'll lend me dayés three,
I'll find a way to make them dee!'

Oh, the first of them was wind and weet;
The second of them was snaw and sleet;
The third of them was sic a freeze,
It froze the wee birds to the trees.

When the three days were past and gane,
The three silly hoggies came hirpling hame!

Lady Day

G. JAMES

Where did Gabriel get a lily,
In the month of March,
  When the green
  Is hardly seen
On the early larch?
  Though I know
  Just where they grow,
I have pulled no daffodilly.
Where did Gabriel get a lily
In the month of March?
  Could I bring
  The tardy spring
Under her foot's arch,
  Near and far,
  The primrose star
Should bloom with violets, willy-nilly.
Where did Gabriel get a lily
In the month of March?

To the Small Celandine

WILLIAM WORDSWORTH

Pansies, lilies, kingcups, daisies,
Let them live upon their praises;
    Long as there's a sun that sets,
        Primroses will have their glory;
    Long as there are violets,
        They will have a place in story:
There's a flower that shall be mine,
'Tis the little Celandine.

Ere a leaf is on a bush,
In the time before the thrush
    Has a thought about her nest,
        Thou wilt come with half a call,
    Spreading out thy glossy breast
        Like a careless Prodigal;
Telling tales about the sun,
When we've little warmth, or none.

Spring

FROM *The Song of Solomon*

For, lo, the winter is past,
The rain is over and gone;
The flowers appear on the earth;
The time of the singing of birds is come,
And the voice of the turtle
    Is heard in our land;
The figtree putteth forth her green figs,
And the vines with the tender grape
        Give a good smell.

21

To Daffodils

ROBERT HERRICK

Fair daffodils, we weep to see
  You haste away so soon;
As yet the early-rising Sun
  Has not attain'd his noon.
    Stay, stay
  Until the hasting day
    Has run
  But to the even song;
And, having pray'd together, we
  Will go with you along.

We have short time to stay, as you,
  We have as short a Spring;
As quick a growth to meet decay,
  As you, or anything.
    We die
  As your hours do, and dry
    Away
  Like to the Summer's rain;
Or as the pearls of morning's dew,
  Ne'er to be found again.

Loveliest of Trees

A. E. HOUSMAN

Loveliest of trees, the cherry now
Is hung with bloom along the bough,
And stands about the woodland ride
Wearing white for Eastertide.

Now, of my threescore years and ten,
Twenty will not come again,
And take from seventy springs a score,
It only leaves me fifty more.

And since to look at things in bloom
Fifty springs are little room,
About the woodlands I will go
To see the cherry hung with snow.

The Calendar

BARBARA EUPHAN TODD

I knew when Spring was come –
Not by the murmurous hum
  Of bees in the willow-trees,
    Or frills
    Of daffodils,
  Or the scent of the breeze;
But because there were whips and tops
By the jars of lollipops
In the two little village shops.

I knew when Summer breathed –
Not by the flowers that wreathed
  The sedge by the water's edge,
    Or gold
    Of the wold,
  Or white and rose of the hedge;
But because, in a wooden box
In the window at Mrs Mock's,
There were white-winged shuttlecocks.

I knew when Autumn came –
Not by the crimson flame
  Of leaves that lapped the eaves
    Or mist
    In amethyst
  And opal-tinted weaves;
But because there were alley-taws
(Punctual as hips and haws)
On the counter at Mrs Shaw's.

I knew when Winter swirled –
Not by the whitened world,
  Or silver skeins in the lanes
    Or frost
    That embossed
  Its patterns on window-panes:
But because there were transfer-sheets
By the bottles of spice and sweets
In the shops in two little streets.

September

MARY COLERIDGE

Now every day the bracken browner grows,
  Even the purple stars
  Of clematis, that shone about the bars,
Grow browner; and the little autumn rose
  Dons, for her rosy gown,
  Sad weeds of brown.

Now falls the eve; and ere the morning sun,
  Many a flower her sweet life will have lost,
  Slain by the bitter frost,
Who slays the butterflies also, one by one,
  The tiny beasts
  That go about their business and their feasts.

To Meadows

ROBERT HERRICK

Ye have been fresh and green,
   Ye have been fill'd with flowers:
And ye the Walks have been
   Where Maids have spent their hours.

You have beheld how they
   With Wicker Arks did come
To kiss and bear away
   The richer Cowslips home.

You've heard them sweetly sing,
   And seen them in a Round:
Each Virgin like a spring,
   With Honeysuckles crown'd.

But now we see none here
   Whose silv'ry feet did tread
And with dishevell'd hair
   Adorn'd this smoother Mead.

Like Unthrifts, having spent
   Your stock and needy grown,
You're left here to lament
   Your poor Estates, alone.

Robin Redbreast

WILLIAM ALLINGHAM

Good-bye, good-bye to Summer!
  For summer's nearly done;
The garden smiling faintly,
  Cool breezes in the sun;
Our thrushes now are silent,
  Our swallows flown away —
But Robin's here in coat of brown,
  And scarlet breast-knot gay.
Robin, Robin Redbreast,
  O Robin dear!
Robin sings so sweetly
  In the falling of the year.

The fireside for the cricket,
  The wheatstack for the mouse,
When trembling night-winds whistle
  And moan all round the house.
The frosty ways like iron,
  The branches plumed with snow.
Alas! in Winter dead and dark,
  Where can poor Robin go?
Robin, Robin Redbreast,
  O Robin dear!
And a crumb of bread for Robin,
  His little heart to cheer.

The North Wind doth Blow

ANONYMOUS

The north wind doth blow,
And we shall have snow,
And what will the robin do then, Poor thing?
    He'll sit in a barn,
    And keep himself warm,
And hide his head under his wing, Poor thing!

The north wind doth blow,
And we shall have snow,
And what will the swallow do then, Poor thing?
    Oh, do you not know
    That he's off long ago,
To a country where he will find spring, Poor thing!

The north wind doth blow,
And we shall have snow,
And what will the dormouse do then, Poor thing?
    Roll'd up like a ball,
    In his nest snug and small,
He'll sleep till warm weather comes in, Poor thing!

The north wind doth blow,
And we shall have snow,
And what will the honey-bee do then, Poor thing?
    In his hive he will stay
    Till the cold is away,
And then he'll come out in the spring, Poor thing!

The north wind doth blow,
And we shall have snow,
And what will the children do then, Poor things?
    When lessons are done,
    They must skip, jump, and run,
Until they have made themselves warm, Poor things!

The Bells

EDGAR ALLAN POE

Hear the sledges with the bells –
    Silver bells!
What a world of merriment their melody foretells!
  How they tinkle, tinkle, tinkle,
    In the icy air of night!
  While the stars that oversprinkle
  All the heavens, seem to twinkle
    With a crystalline delight;
  Keeping time, time, time,
  In a sort of Runic rhyme,
To the tintinabulation that so musically wells
From the bells, bells, bells, bells,
    Bells, bells, bells –
From the jingling and the tinkling of the bells.

Blow, Blow, thou Winter Wind

WILLIAM SHAKESPEARE

Blow, blow, thou Winter wind,
Thou art not so unkind
  As man's ingratitude;
Thy tooth is not so keen,
Because thou art not seen,
  Although thy breath be rude.
Heigh ho! sing heigh ho! unto the green holly;
Most friendship is feigning, most loving mere folly:
  Then heigh ho, the holly!
  This life is most jolly.

Freeze, freeze, thou bitter sky,
Thou dost not bite so nigh
  As benefits forgot;
Though thou the waters warp,
Thy sting is not so sharp
  As friend remembered not.
Heigh ho! sing heigh ho! unto the green holly;
Most friendship is feigning, most loving mere folly:
  Then heigh ho, the holly!
  This life is most jolly.

Spring Quiet

CHRISTINA ROSSETTI

Gone were but the Winter,
    Come were but the Spring,
I would go to a covert
    Where the birds sing.

Where in the whitethorn
    Singeth a thrush,
And a robin sings
    In the holly-bush.

Full of fresh scents
    Are the budding boughs
Arching high over
    A cool green house:

Full of sweet scents,
    And whispering air
Which sayeth softly:
    'We spread no snare;

'Here dwell in safety,
    Here dwell alone,
With a clear stream
    And a mossy stone.

'Here the sun shineth
    Most shadily;
Here is heard an echo
    Of the far sea,
    Though far off it be.'

Faery Song

JOHN KEATS

Shed no tear! Oh shed no tear!
The flower will bloom another year.
Weep no more! Oh weep no more!
Young buds sleep in the root's white core.
Dry your eyes! Oh dry your eyes!
For I was taught in Paradise
To ease my breast of melodies –
  Shed no tear.

Overhead! look overhead!
'Mong the blossoms white and red –
Look up, look up. I flutter now
On this flush pomegranite bough.
See me! 'tis this silvery bill
Ever cures the good man's ill.
Shed no tear! Oh shed no tear!
The flower will bloom another year.
Adieu, Adieu! I fly, adieu!
I vanish in the heaven's blue –
  Adieu, Adieu!

2 · OF BIRDS AND BEASTS

—

The Clucking Hen

A. HAWKSHAWE

'Pray will you take a walk with me,
  My little wife, to-day?
There's barley in the barley fields,
  And hay-seeds in the hay.'

'Thank you,' said the clucking hen,
  'I've something else to do.
I'm busy sitting on my eggs;
  I cannot walk with you.'

The clucking hen sat on her nest,
  She made it in the hay;
And warm and snug beneath her breast,
  A dozen white eggs lay.

'CRACK CRACK' went all the little eggs,
  'CHEEP CHEEP' the chickens small!
'CLUCK!' said the clucking hen,
  'Now I have you all.'

'Now come along, my little chicks,
  I'll take a walk with YOU.'
'Hullo,' then crowed the barn-door cock,
  And 'cockadoodle doo!'

Three Limericks

EDWARD LEAR

There was an Old Man who said, 'How
Shall I flee from that horrible cow?
   I will sit on this stile,
   And continue to smile,
Which may soften the heart of that cow.

*   *   *

There was an Old Man in a tree,
Who was horribly bored by a bee.
   When they said, 'Does it buzz?'
   He replied, 'Yes, it does!
It's a regular brute of a bee!'

*   *   *

There was an Old Man who said, 'Hush!
I perceive a young bird in this bush.'
   When they said, 'Is it small?'
   He replied, 'Not at all!
It is four times as big as the bush.'

Natural History

ADELAIDE O'KEEFE

The Dog will come when he is called,
   The Cat will walk away.
The Monkey's cheek is very bald,
   The Goat is fond of play.
The Parrot is a prate-apace,
Yet I know not what he says,
The noble Horse will win the race
   Or draw you in a chaise.

The Pig is not a feeder nice,
   The Squirrel loves a nut,
The Wolf would eat you in a trice,
   The Buzzard's eyes are shut.
The Lark sings high up in the air,
The Linnet in the tree;
The Swan he has a bosom fair,
   And who so proud as he?

Who Killed Cock Robin?

ANONYMOUS

Who killed Cock Robin?
  I, said the Sparrow,
    With my bow and arrow,
I killed Cock Robin.

Who saw him die?
  I, said the Fly.
    With my little eye,
I saw him die.

Who caught his blood?
  I, said the Fish,
    With my little dish,
I caught his blood.

Who'll make his shroud?
  I, said the Beetle,
    With my thread and needle,
I'll make his shroud.

Who'll dig his grave?
  I, said the Owl,
    With my spade and trowel,
I'll dig his grave.

Who'll carry the link?
  I, said the Linnet,
    I'll come in a minute,
I'll bear the link.

Who'll be the parson?
  I, said the Rook,
  With my little book.
I'll be the parson.

Who'll carry him to his grave?
  I, said the Kite,
  If it's not in the night,
I'll carry him to the grave.

Who'll be chief mourner?
  I, said the Dove,
  I mourn for my love.
I'll be chief mourner.

Who'll bear the pall?
  We, said the Wren,
  Both the cock and the hen,
We'll bear the pall.

Who'll sing a psalm?
  I said the Thrush,
  As she sat in a bush,
I'll sing a psalm.

Who'll toll the bell?
  I, said the Bull,
  Because I can pull,
I'll toll the bell.

  And so Robin, Farewell!

And all the birds of the air
Fell a-sighing and a-sobbing,
When they heard of the death
  Of poor Cock Robin.

The Robin and the Wren

ANONYMOUS

The robin and the redbreast,
    The robin and the wren,
If you take them out of their nest,
    Ye'll ne'er thrive again.

The robin and the redbreast,
    The martin and the swallow;
If you touch one of their eggs,
    Ill luck is sure to follow.

Scottish Nursery Rhyme

ANONYMOUS

There was a wee bit mousikie,
    That lived in Gilberaty-O,
It couldno' get a bite o' cheese,
    For cheatie pussy-catty-O.

It said unto the cheeseky,
    'Oh fain would I be at ye-O,
If 'twere no' for the cruel claws
    Of cheatie pussy-catty-O.'

He! Haw! Hum!

ANONYMOUS

John Cook had a little grey mare,
   He haw hum!
Her back stood up and her bones were bare.
   He haw hum.

John Cook was riding up Shuter's Bank,
   He haw hum!
And there his nag did kick and prank.
   He haw hum.

John Cook was riding up Shuter's Hill,
   He haw hum!
His mare fell down and she made her will!
   He haw hum.

The bridle and saddle were laid on the shelf.
   He haw hum.
If you want any more, you must make it yourself.
   He haw hum.

I had a little Pony

ANONYMOUS

I had a little pony
   His name was Dapple-grey
I lent him to a lady,
   To ride a mile away.

She whipped him, she lashed him,
   She drove him through the mire.
I wouldn't lend my pony now,
   For all the lady's hire.

Lone Dog

IRENE MCLEOD

I'm a lean dog, a keen dog, a wild dog and lone,
I'm a rough dog, a tough dog, hunting on my own!
I'm a bad dog, a mad dog, teasing silly sheep;
I love to sit and bay the moon and keep fat souls from sleep.

I'll never be a lap dog, licking dirty feet,
A sleek dog, a meek dog, cringing for my meat.
Not for me the fireside, the well-filled plate,
But shut door and sharp stone and cuff and kick and hate.

Not for me the other dogs, running by my side,
Some have run a short while, but none of them would bide.
O mine is still the lone trail, the hard trail, the best,
Wide wind and wild stars and the hunger of the quest.

Little Trotty Wagtail

JOHN CLARE

Little Trotty Wagtail, he went in the rain,
And twittering, tottering sideways, he ne'er got straight again;
He stooped to get a worm, and looked up to get a fly,
And then he flew away ere his feathers they were dry.

Little Trotty Wagtail, he waddled in the mud,
And left his little foot-marks, trample where he would,
He waddled in the water-pudge, and waggle went his tail,
And chirrupped up his wings to dry upon the garden rail.

Little Trotty Wagtail, you nimble all about,
And in the dimpling water-pudge you waddle in and out:
Your home is nigh at hand and in the warm pig-stye;
So, little Master Wagtail, I'll bid you a good-bye.

What can Lambkins do?

CHRISTINA ROSSETTI

What can lambkins do
All the keen night through?
Nestle by their woolly mother,
The careful ewe.

What can nestlings do
In the nightly dew?
Sleep beneath their mother's wing
Till day breaks anew.

If in field or tree
There might only be
Such a warm soft sleeping-place
Found for me!

The Mouse

ELIZABETH COATSWORTH

I hear a mouse
Bitterly complaining
In a crack of moonlight
Aslant on the floor –

'Little I ask
And that little is not granted.
There are few crumbs
In this world any more.

'The breadbox is tin
And I cannot get in.

'The jam's in a jar
My teeth cannot mar.

'The cheese sits by itself
On the pantry shelf.

'All night I run
Searching and seeking,
All night I run
About on the floor.

'Moonlight is there
And a bare place for dancing,
But no little feast
Is spread any more.'

The Cow

ROBERT LOUIS STEVENSON

The friendly cow all red and white,
   I love with all my heart:
She gives me cream with all her might,
   To eat with apple-tart.

She wanders lowing here and there,
   And yet she cannot stray,
All in the pleasant open air,
   The pleasant light of day;

And blown by all the winds that pass
   And wet with all the showers,
She walks among the meadow grass
   And eats the meadow flowers.

The Fly

WILLIAM BLAKE

Little Fly,
Thy summer's play
My thoughtless hand
Has brushed away.

Am not I
A fly like thee?
Or art not thou
A man like me?

For I dance,
And drink, and sing,
Till some blind hand
Shall brush my wing.

If thought is life
And strength and breath,
And the want
Of thought is death;

Then am I
A happy fly,
If I live
Or if I die.

The Kitten and the Falling Leaves

WILLIAM WORDSWORTH

See the Kitten on the wall,
Sporting with the leaves that fall,
Withered leaves – one, two and three –
From the lofty elder-tree!
Through the calm and frosty air
Of this morning bright and fair,
Eddying round and round they sink
Softly, slowly: one might think,
From the motions that are made,
Every little leaf conveyed
Sylph or Faery hither tending,
To this lower world descending,
Each invisible and mute,
In his wavering parachute.

– But the Kitten, how she starts,
Crouches, stretches paws, and darts!
First at one, and then its fellow
Just as light and just as yellow.
There are many now – now one –
Now they stop and there are none:

What intenseness of desire
In her upward eye of fire!
With a tiger-leap half way
Now she meets the coming prey,
Lets it go as fast, and then
Has it in her power again:

Now she works with three or four,
Like an Indian conjurer;
Quick as he in feats of art,
Far beyond in joy of heart.
Were her antics played in the eye
Of a thousand standers-by,
Clapping hands with shout and stare,
What would little Tabby care
For the plaudits of the crowd?

Mister Fox

ANONYMOUS

A fox went out in a hungry plight,
And he begged of the moon to give him light,
For he'd many miles to trot that night,
 Before he could reach his den O!

And first he came to a farmer's yard,
Where the ducks and geese declared it hard
That their nerves should be shaken and their rest be marr'd,
 By the visit of Mister Fox O!

He took the grey goose by the sleeve;
Says he, 'Madam Goose, and by your leave,
I'll take you away without reprieve,
 And carry you home to my den O!'

He seized the black duck by the neck,
And swung her over across his back;
The black duck cried out, 'Quack! Quack! Quack!'
 With her legs hanging dangling down O!

Then old Mrs Slipper-slopper jump'd out of bed,
And out of the window she popp'd her head,
Crying, 'John, John, John, the grey goose is gone,
 And the fox is away to his den O!'

Then John he went up to the top of the hill,
And he blew a blast both loud and shrill;
Says the fox, 'That is very pretty music – still
 I'd rather be in my den O!'

At last the fox got home to his den;
To his dear little foxes, eight, nine, ten,
Says he, 'You're in luck, here's a good fat duck,
 With her legs hanging dangling down O!'

He then sat down with his hungry wife;
They did very well without fork or knife;
They'd never ate better in all their life,
 And the little ones pick'd the bones O!

The Tyger

WILLIAM BLAKE

Tyger! Tyger! burning bright
In the forests of the night,
What immortal hand or eye
Could frame thy fearful symmetry?

In what distant deeps or skies
Burnt the fire of thine eyes?
On what wings dare he aspire?
What the hand dare seize the fire?

And what shoulder, and what art,
Could twist the sinews of thy heart?
And, when thy heart began to beat,
What dread hand? and what dread feet?

What the hammer? what the chain?
In what furnace was thy brain?
What the anvil? what dread grasp
Dare its deadly terrors clasp?

When the stars threw down their spears,
And water'd heaven with their tears,
Did he smile his work to see?
Did he who made the Lamb make thee?

Tyger! Tyger! burning bright
In the forests of the night,
What immortal hand or eye,
Dare frame thy fearful symmetry?

Answer to a Child's Question

SAMUEL TAYLOR COLERIDGE

Do you ask what the birds say? The sparrow, the dove,
The linnet and thrush say, 'I love and I love!'
In the winter they're silent, the wind is so strong;
What it says I don't know, but it sings a loud song.
But green leaves, and blossoms, and sunny warm weather,
And singing and loving – all come back together.
But the lark is so brimful of gladness and love,
The green fields below him, the blue sky above,
That he sings, and he sings, and for ever sings he,
'I love my Love, and my Love loves me.'

To a Butterfly

WILLIAM WORDSWORTH

I've watched you now a full half-hour,
Self-poised upon that yellow flower;
And, little Butterfly! indeed
I know not if you sleep or feed.
How motionless! – not frozen seas
More motionless! And then
What joy awaits you, when the breeze
Hath found you out among the trees,
And calls you forth again!

This plot of orchard-ground is ours;
My trees they are, my Sister's flowers.
Here rest your wings when they are weary;
Here lodge as in a sanctuary!
Come often to us, fear no wrong;
Sit near us on the bough!
We'll talk of sunshine and of song,
And summer days, when we were young;
Sweet childish days, that were as long
As twenty days are now.

Epitaph on a Hare

WILLIAM COWPER

Here lies, whom hound did ne'er pursue,
　Nor swifter greyhound follow,
Whose foot ne'er tainted morning dew,
　Nor ear heard huntsman's hollo,

Old Tiney, surliest of his kind,
　Who, nursed with tender care,
And to domestic bounds confined,
　Was still a wild Jack-hare.

Though duly from my hand he took
　His pittance every night,
He did it with a jealous look,
　And, when he could, would bite.

His diet was of wheaten bread,
　And milk, and oats, and straw,
Thistles, or lettuces instead,
　With sand to scour his maw.

On twigs of hawthorn he regaled,
　On pippins' russet peel;
And, when his juicy salads failed,
　Sliced carrot pleased him well.

A Turkey carpet was his lawn,
　Whereon he loved to bound,
To skip and gambol like a fawn,
　And swing his rump around.

His frisking was at evening hours,
   For then he lost his fear;
But most before approaching showers,
   Or when a storm drew near.

Eight years and five round-rolling moons
   He thus saw steal away,
Dozing out all his idle noons,
   And every night at play.

I kept him for his humour's sake,
   For he would oft beguile
My heart of thoughts that made it ache,
   And force me to a smile.

But now, beneath this walnut-shade,
   He finds his long, last home,
And waits, in snug concealment laid,
   Till gentler Puss shall come.

He, still more aged, feels the shocks
   From which no care can save,
And, partner once of Tiney's box,
   Must soon partake his grave.

Hiawatha's Childhood

HENRY WADSWORTH LONGFELLOW

Then the little Hiawatha
Learned of every bird its language,
Learned their names and all their secrets:
How they built their nests in Summer,
Where they hid themselves in Winter,
Talked with them whene'er he met them,
Called them 'Hiawatha's Chickens'.

Of all the beasts he learned the language,
Learned their names and all their secrets,
How the beavers built their lodges,
How the squirrels hid their acorns,
How the reindeer ran so swiftly,
Why the rabbit was so timid;
Talked with them whene'er he met them,
Called them 'Hiawatha's Brothers'.

Then Iagoo, the great boaster,
He the marvellous story-teller,
He the traveller and the talker,
He the friend of old Nokomis,
Made a bow for Hiawatha:
From a branch of ash he made it,
From an oak-bough made the arrows,
Tipped with flint, and winged with feathers,
And the cord he made of deer-skin.

Then he said to Hiawatha:
'Go, my son, into the forest,
Where the red deer herd together,
Kill for us a famous roebuck,
Kill for us a deer with antlers!'

Forth into the forest straightway
All alone walked Hiawatha
Proudly, with his bows and arrows;
And the birds sang round him, o'er him,
'Do not shoot us, Hiawatha!'
Sang the robin, the Opechee,
Sang the bluebird, the Owaissa,
'Do not shoot us, Hiawatha!'

Up the oak-tree, close beside him,
Sprang the squirrel, Adjidaumo,
In and out among the branches,
Coughed and chattered from the oak-tree,
Laughed, and said between his laughing,
'Do not shoot me, Hiawatha!'

And the rabbit from his pathway
Leaped aside, and at a distance
Sat erect upon his haunches,
Half in fear and half in frolic,
Saying to the little hunter,
'Do not shoot me, Hiawatha!'

But he heeded not, nor heard them,
For his thoughts were with the red deer;
On their tracks his eyes were fastened,
Leading downward to the river,
To the ford across the river,
And as one in slumber walked he.

Hidden in the alder-bushes,
There he waited till the deer came,
Till he saw two antlers lifted,
Saw two eyes look from the thicket,
Saw two nostrils point to windward,

And a deer came down the pathway,
Flecked with leafy light and shadow;
And his heart within him fluttered,
Trembled like the leaves above him,
Like the birch-leaf palpitated,
As the deer came down the pathway.

Then, upon one knee uprising,
Hiawatha aimed an arrow;
Scarce a twig moved with his motion,
Scarce a leaf was stirred or rustled,
But the wary roebuck started,
Stamped with all his hoofs together,
Listened with one foot uplifted,
Leaped as if to meet the arrow;
Ah the singing, fatal arrow,
Like a wasp it buzzed and stung him.

Dead he lay there in the forest
By the ford across the river;
Beat his timid heart no longer;
But the heart of Hiawatha
Throbbed and shouted and exulted,
As he bore the red deer homeward;
But Iagoo and Nokomis
Hailed his coming with applauses.

From the red deer's hide, Nokomis
Made a cloak for Hiawatha;
From the deer's flesh Nokomis
Made a banquet in his honour.
All the village came and feasted,
All the guests praised Hiawatha,
Called him Strong-Heart, Soan-getaha!
Called him Loon-heart, Mahn-go-taysee!

Auguries of Innocence

WILLIAM BLAKE

To see a World in a Grain of Sand,
And a Heaven in a Wild Flower,
Hold Infinity in the palm of your hand,
And Eternity in an hour.

A Robin Redbreast in a Cage
Puts all Heaven in a Rage.
A dove-house fill'd with Doves and Pigeons
Shudders Hell thro' all its regions.

A dog starv'd at his Master's Gate
Predicts the ruin of the State
A Horse misused upon the Road
Calls to Heaven for Human blood.

Each outcry of the hunted Hare
A fibre from the Brain does tear.
A Skylark wounded in the wing;
A Cherubim does cease to sing.

The Game Cock clipt and arm'd for fight
Does the Rising Sun affright.
Every Wolf's and Lion's howl
Raises from Hell a Human Soul.

The wild Deer, wand'ring here and there,
Keeps the Human Soul from Care.
The Lamb misus'd breeds Public Strife,
And yet forgives the Butcher's Knife.

The Bat that flits at close of Eve
Has left the Brain that won't Believe.
The Owl that calls upon the Night
Speaks the Unbeliever's fright.

He who shall hurt the little Wren
Shall never be belov'd by Men.
He who the Ox to wrath has mov'd
Shall never be by Woman lov'd.

The wanton Boy that kills the Fly
Shall feel the Spider's enmity....
The Beggar's Dog and Widow's Cat,
Feed them and thou wilt grow fat.

A Truth that's told with bad intent
Beats all the Lies you can invent.
It is right it should be so;
Man was made for Joy and Woe;
And when this we rightly know,
Thro' the World we safely go.

Joy and Woe are woven fine,
A Clothing for the soul divine;
Under every grief and pine
Runs a joy with silken twine.

The Babe is more than Swadling Bands;
Throughout all these Human Lands
Tools were made, and Born were hands,
Every Farmer understands.

Every Night and every Morn
Some to Misery are born.
Every Morn and every Night
Some are Born to Sweet Delight.
Some are Born to Sweet Delight,
Some are Born to Endless Night.

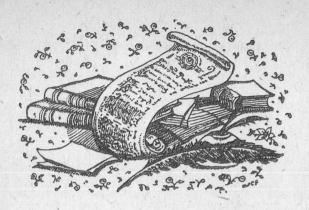

3 · BALLADS AND STORIES

—

The Babes in the Wood · *Anonymous*
John Gilpin · *William Cowper*
Humpty Dumpty's Poem · *Lewis Carroll*
The Jumblies · *Edward Lear*
The Pobble who has no Toes · *Edward Lear*
Lucy Gray – or Solitude · *William Wordsworth*
Hall and Knight · *E. V. Rieu*
Eldorado · *Edgar Allan Poe*
The Revenge, A Ballad of the Fleet · *Alfred Lord Tennyson*
Lochinvar · *Sir Walter Scott*
Thomas the Rhymer · *Anonymous*
The Bonny Earl of Moray · *Anonymous*
The Twa Corbies · *Anonymous*
Sir Patrick Spens · *Anonymous*
King John and the Abbot of Canterbury · *Anonymous*
La Belle Dame Sans Merci · *John Keats*
The Secret · *Anonymous*
From The Leech Gatherer · *William Wordsworth*
Token of All Brave Captains · *Captain Marryat*
Little Billee · *William Makepeace Thackeray*
The Raiders · *Will H. Ogilvie*

The Babes in the Wood

ANONYMOUS

My dear, do you know
How a long time ago,
   Two poor little children,
Whose names I don't know,
Were stolen away
On a fine summer's day,
   And left in a wood,
As I've heard people say.

And when it was night,
So sad was their plight,
   The sun it went down,
And the moon gave no light!
They sobbed and they sighed,
And they bitterly cried,
   And the poor little things,
They lay down and died.

And when they were dead,
The robins so red
   Brought strawberry leaves
And over them spread;
And all the day long,
They sang them this song –
   Poor babes in the wood!
   Poor babes in the wood!
And won't you remember
   The babes in the wood?

The Diverting History of John Gilpin

Showing how he went farther than he intended, and came safe home again

WILLIAM COWPER

John Gilpin was a citizen
    Of credit and renown,
A train band captain eke was he
    Of famous London town.

John Gilpin's spouse said to her dear,
    'Though wedded we have been
These twice ten tedious years, yet we
    No holiday have seen.

'To-morrow is our wedding day,
    And we will then repair
Unto the Bell at Edmonton,
    All in a chaise and pair.

'My sister and my sister's child,
    Myself and children three,
Will fill the chaise; so you must ride
    On horseback after we.'

He soon replied, 'I do admire
    Of womankind but one,
And you are she, my dearest dear,
    Therefore it shall be done.

'I am a linen draper bold,
    As all the world doth know,
And my good friend, the calender,
    Will lend his horse to go.'

Quoth Mrs Gilpin, 'That's well said;
    And, for that wine is dear,
We will be furnished with our own,
    Which is both bright and clear.'

John Gilpin kissed his loving wife;
    O'erjoyed was he to find,
That though on pleasure she was bent,
    She had a frugal mind.

The morning came, the chaise was brought,
    But yet was not allowed
To drive up to the door, lest all
    Should say that she was proud.

So three doors off the chaise was stayed,
    Where they did all get in;
Six precious souls, and all agog
    To dash through thick and thin.

Smack went the whip, round went the wheels,
    Were never folk so glad;
The stones did rattle underneath,
    As if Cheapside were mad.

John Gilpin at his horse's side
    Seized the fast flowing mane,
And up he got, in haste to ride,
    But soon came down again:

For saddle tree scarce reached had he,
    His journey to begin,
When, turning round his head, he saw
    Three customers come in.

So down he came; for loss of time,
　　Although it grieved him sore,
Yet loss of pence, full well he knew,
　　Would trouble him much more.

'Twas long before the customers
　　Were suited to their mind,
When Betty, screaming, came downstairs,
　　'The wine is left behind!'

'Good lack!' quoth he, 'yet bring it me,
　　My leathern belt likewise,
In which I bear my trusty sword
　　When I do exercise!'

Now mistress Gilpin (careful soul!)
　　Had two stone bottles found,
To hold the liquor that she loved,
　　And keep it safe and sound.

Each bottle had a curling ear,
　　Through which the belt he drew,
And hung a bottle on each side,
　　To make his balance true.

Then, over all, that he might be
　　Equipped from top to toe,
His long red cloak, well brushed and neat,
　　He manfully did throw.

Now see him mounted once again
　　Upon his nimble steed,
Full slowly pacing o'er the stones,
　　With caution and good heed.

But finding soon a smoother road
    Beneath his well-shod feet,
The snorting beast began to trot,
    Which galled him in his seat.

So, 'Fair and softly!' John he cried,
    But John he cried in vain.
That trot became a gallop soon,
    In spite of curb and rein.

So, stooping down, as needs he must
    Who cannot sit upright,
He grasped the mane with both his hands,
    And eke with all his might.

His horse, who never in that sort
    Had handled been before,
What thing upon his back had got
    Did wonder more and more.

Away went Gilpin, neck or nought;
    Away went hat and wig;
He little dreamt when he set out,
    Of running such a rig.

The wind did blow, the cloak did fly,
    Like streamer long and gay,
Till, loop and button failing both,
    At last it flew away.

Then might all people well discern
    The bottles he had slung;
A bottle swinging at each side,
    As hath been said or sung.

The dogs did bark, the children screamed,
  Up flew the windows all;
And every soul cried out, 'Well done!'
  As loud as he could bawl.

Away went Gilpin – who but he?
  His fame soon spread around –
'He carries weight!' 'He rides a race!'
' 'Tis for a thousand pound!'

And still, as fast as he drew near,
  'Twas wonderful to view,
How in a trice the turnpike-men
  Their gates wide open threw.

And now, as he went bowing down
  His reeking head full low,
The bottles twain behind his back
  Were shattered at a blow.

Down ran the wine into the road,
  Most piteous to be seen,
Which made his horse's flanks to smoke
  As they had basted been.

But still he seemed to carry weight,
  With leathern girdle braced;
For all might see the bottle necks
  Still dangling at his waist.

Thus all through merry Islington
  These gambols he did play,
Until he came unto the Wash
  Of Edmonton so gay;

And there he threw the wash about
   On both sides of the way,
Just like unto a trundling mop,
   Or a wild goose at play.

At Edmonton, his loving wife
   From the balcony espied
Her tender husband, wondering much
   To see how he did ride.

'Stop, stop, John Gilpin! Here's the house!'
   They all at once did cry;
'The dinner waits, and we are tired!'
   Said Gilpin, 'So am I!'

But yet his horse was not a whit
   Inclined to tarry there.
For why? His owner had a house
   Full ten miles off, at Ware.

So, like an arrow swift he flew,
   Shot by an archer strong.
So did he fly – which brings me to
   The middle of my song.

Away went Gilpin, out of breath,
   And sore against his will,
Till, at his friend the calender's,
   His horse at last stood still.

The calender, amazed to see
   His neighbour in such trim,
Laid down his pipe, flew to the gate,
   And thus accosted him:

'What news? What news? Your tidings tell,
  Tell me you must and shall –
Say why bare-headed you are come,
  Or why you come at all?'

Now Gilpin had a pleasant wit,
  And loved a timely joke;
And thus unto the calender
  In merry guise he spoke:

'I came because your horse would come,
  And, if I well forebode,
My hat and wig will soon be here,
  They are upon the road.'

The calender, right glad to find
  His friend in merry pin,
Returned him not a single word,
  But to the house went in;

Whence straight he came with hat and wig,
  A wig that flowed behind,
A hat not much the worse for wear,
  Each comely in its kind.

He held them up, and in his turn
  Thus showed his ready wit,
'My head is twice as big as yours,
  They therefore needs must fit.

'But let me scrape the dirt away
  That hangs upon your face;
And stop and eat, for well you may
  Be in a hungry case.'

Said John, 'It is my wedding day,
   And all the world would stare,
If wife should dine at Edmonton,
   And I should dine at Ware.'

So, turning to his horse, he said,
   'I am in haste to dine;
'Twas for your pleasure you came here,
   You shall go back for mine.'

Ah luckless speech, and bootless boast!
   For which he paid full dear;
For, while he spake, a braying ass
   Did sing most loud and clear;

Whereat his horse did snort, as he
   Had heard a lion roar,
And galloped off with all his might,
   As he had done before.

Away went Gilpin, and away
   Went Gilpin's hat and wig.
He lost them sooner than at first;
   For why? They were too big.

Now mistress Gilpin, when she saw
   Her husband posting down
Into the country far away
   She pulled out half-a-crown;

And thus unto the youth she said,
   That drove them to the Bell:
'This shall be yours, when you bring back
   My husband safe and well.'

The youth did ride, and soon did meet
   John coming back amain;

Whom in a trice he tried to stop,
   By catching at the rein.

But, not performing what he meant
   And gladly would have done,
The frightened steed he frighted more,
   And made him faster run.

Away went Gilpin, and away
   Went postboy at his heels.
The postboy's horse right glad to miss
   The lumbering of the wheels.

Six gentlemen upon the road,
   Thus seeing Gilpin fly,
With postboy scampering in the rear,
   They raised the hue and cry:

'Stop thief! Stop thief!' – 'A highwayman!'
   Not one of them was mute;
And all and each that passed that way
   Did join in the pursuit.

And now the turnpike gates again
   Flew open in short space;
The toll-men thinking, as before,
   That Gilpin rode a race.

And so he did, and won it too,
   For he got first to town;
Nor stopped till where he had got up
   He did again get down.

Now let us sing, Long live the King!
   And Gilpin, long live he!
And when he next doth ride abroad,
   May I be there to see.

Humpty Dumpty's Poem

LEWIS CARROLL

In winter, when the fields are white,
I sing this song for your delight –

In spring, when woods are getting green,
I'll try and tell you what I mean.

In summer, when the days are long,
Perhaps you'll understand the song:

In autumn, when the leaves are brown,
Take pen and ink, and write it down.

I sent a message to the fish:
I told them 'This is what I wish.'

The little fishes of the sea,
They sent an answer back to me.

The little fishes' answer was
'We cannot do it, Sir, because – '

I sent to them again to say
'It will be better to obey.'

The fishes answered with a grin,
'Why, what a temper you are in!'

I told them once, I told them twice:
They would not listen to advice.

I took a kettle large and new,
Fit for the deed I had to do.

My heart went hop, my heart went thump;
I filled the kettle at the pump.

Then someone came to me and said,
'The little fishes are in bed.'

I said to him, I said it plain,
'Then you must wake them up again.'

I said it very loud and clear;
I went and shouted in his ear.

But he was very stiff and proud;
He said 'You needn't shout so loud!'

And he was very proud and stiff;
He said 'I'd go and wake them, if –'

I took a corkscrew from the shelf:
I went to wake them up myself.

And when I found the door was locked,
I pulled and pushed and kicked and knocked.

And when I found the door was shut,
I tried to turn the handle, but –

The Jumblies

EDWARD LEAR

They went to sea in a Sieve, they did,
  In a Sieve they went to sea;
In spite of all their friends could say,
On a winter's morn, on a stormy day,
  In a Sieve they went to sea!
And when the Sieve turned round and round,
And everyone cried, 'You'll all be drowned!'
They called aloud, 'Our Sieve ain't big,
But we don't care a button, we don't care a fig!
  In a Sieve we'll go to sea.'
    Far and few, far and few,
      Are the lands where the Jumblies live;
      Their heads are green, and their hands are blue,
      And they went to sea in a Sieve.

They sailed away in a Sieve, they did,
  In a Sieve they sailed so fast;
With only a beautiful pea-green veil
Tied with a riband by way of a sail
  To a small tobacco-pipe mast;
And everyone said, who saw them go,
'O won't they be soon upset, you know,
For the sky is dark, and the voyage is long,
And happen what may, it's extremely wrong,
  In a Sieve to sail so fast.'
    Far and few, far and few,
      Are the lands where the Jumblies live;
      Their heads are green, and their hands are blue,
      And they went to sea in a Sieve.

The water it soon came in, it did,
   The water it soon came in;
So to keep them dry, they wrapped their feet
In a pinky paper, all folded neat,
   And they fastened it down with a pin.
And they passed the night in a crockery jar,
And each of them said, 'How wise we are!
Though the sky be dark and the voyage be long
Yet we never can think we were rash or wrong,
   While round in our Sieve we spin!'
     Far and few, far and few,
       Are the lands where the Jumblies live;
       Their heads are green, and their hands are blue,
       And they went to sea in a Sieve.

And all night long they sailed away;
   And when the sun went down,
They whistled and warbled a moony song,
To the echoing sound of a coppery gong,
   In the shade of the mountains brown.
'O Timballo! How happy we are,
When we live in a Sieve and a crockery jar,
And all night long in the moonlight pale,
We sail away with a pea-green sail
   In the shade of the mountains brown!'
     Far and few, far and few,
       Are the lands where the Jumblies live;
       Their heads are green, and their hands are blue,
       And they went to sea in a Sieve.

They sailed to the Western Sea, they did,
   To a land all covered with trees,
And they bought an Owl and a useful Cart,
And a pound of Rice and a Cranberry Tart,
   And a hive of silvery Bees.
And they bought a Pig, and some green Jack-daws,
And a lovely Monkey with lollipop paws,
And forty bottles of Ring-Bo-Ree,
   And no end of Stilton Cheese.
     Far and few, far and few,
       Are the lands where the Jumblies live;
      Their heads are green, and their hands are blue,
       And they went to sea in a Sieve.

And in twenty years they all came back,
   In twenty years or more.
And everyone said, 'How tall they've grown!
For they've been to the Lakes, and the Torrible Zone,
   And the hills of the Chankly Bore;'
And they drank their health and gave them a feast
Of dumplings made of beautiful yeast;
And everyone said, 'If we only live,
We, too, will go to sea in a Sieve –
   To the hills of the Chankly Bore!'
     Far and few, far and few,
       Are the lands where the Jumblies live;
      Their heads are green, and their hands are blue,
       And they went to sea in a Sieve.

The Pobble who has no Toes

EDWARD LEAR

The Pobble who has no toes,
    Had once as many as we;
When they said, 'Some day you may lose them all;'
    He replied, 'Fish, fiddle-de-dee!'
And his Aunt Jobiska made him drink
Lavender water tinged with pink,
For she said, 'The World in general knows
There's nothing so good for a Pobble's toes!'

The Pobble who has no toes
    Swam across the Bristol Channel;
But before he set out he wrapped his nose
    In a piece of scarlet flannel.
For his Aunt Jobiska said, 'No harm
Can come to his toes if his nose is warm;
And it's perfectly known that a Pobble's toes
Are safe – provided he minds his nose!'

The Pobble swam fast and well
    And when boats or ships came near him,
He tinkledy-binkledy-winkled a bell,
    So that all the world could hear him.
And all the Sailors and Admirals cried –
When they saw him nearing the further side –
'He has gone to fish for his Aunt Jobiska's
Runcible Cat with crimson whiskers!'

But before he touched the shore,
    The shore of the Bristol Channel,
A sea-green Porpoise carried away
    His wrapper of scarlet flannel.
And when he came to observe his feet,
Formerly garnished with toes so neat,
His face at once became forlorn,
On perceiving that all his toes were gone!

And nobody ever knew,
    From that dark day to the present,
Whoso had taken the Pobble's toes,
    In a manner so far from pleasant.
Whether the shrimps or crawfish grey
Or crafty Mermaids stole them away —
Nobody knew: and nobody knows
How the Pobble was robbed of his twice five toes!

The Pobble who has no toes
    Was placed in a friendly Bark,
And they rowed him back, and carried him up
    To his Aunt Jobiska's Park.
And she made him a feast at his earnest wish
Of eggs and buttercups fried with fish —
And she said — 'It's a fact the whole world knows
That Pobbles are happier without their toes!'

Lucy Gray – or Solitude

WILLIAM WORDSWORTH

Oft I had heard of Lucy Gray:
  And, when I crossed the wild,
I chanced to see at break of day
  The solitary child.

No mate, no comrade Lucy knew;
  She dwelt on a wide moor,
The sweetest thing that ever grew
  Beside a human door!

You yet may spy the fawn at play,
  The hare upon the green;
But the sweet face of Lucy Gray
  Will never more be seen.

'To-night will be a stormy night
  You to the town must go;
And take a lantern, Child, to light
  Your mother through the snow.'

'That, Father, will I gladly do:
  'Tis scarcely afternoon –
The minster-clock has just struck two,
  And yonder is the moon!'

At this the father raised his hook
  And snapped a faggot-band;
He plied his work; and Lucy took
  The lantern in her hand.

Not blither is the mountain roe:
  With many a wanton stroke
Her feet disperse the powdery snow,
  That rises up like smoke.

The storm came on before its time:
  She wandered up and down;
And many a hill did Lucy climb:
  But never reached the town.

The wretched parents all that night
  Went shouting far and wide;
But there was neither sound nor sight
  To serve them for a guide.

At daybreak on a hill they stood
  That overlooked the moor;
And thence they saw the bridge of wood,
  A furlong from their door.

They wept – and, turning homeward, cried
  'In heaven we all shall meet!'
When in the snow the mother spied
  The print of Lucy's feet.

Then downwards from the steep hill's edge
  They tracked the footmarks small;
And through the broken hawthorn hedge,
  And by the long stone-wall;

And then an open field they crossed:
  The marks were still the same;
They tracked them on, nor ever lost;
  And to the bridge they came.

They followed from the snowy bank
  Those footmarks, one by one,
Into the middle of the plank;
  And further were there none!

Yet some maintain that to this day
   She is a living child;
That you may see sweet Lucy Gray
   Upon the lonesome wild.

O'er rough and smooth she trips along,
   And never looks behind;
And sings a solitary song
   That whistles in the wind.

Hall and Knight

OR

$$z + b + x = y + b + z$$

E. V. RIEU

When he was young his cousins used to say of Mr Knight:
'This boy will write an Algebra – or looks as if he might.'
And sure enough, when Mr Knight had grown to be a man,
He purchased pen and paper and an inkpot, and began.

But he very soon discovered that he couldn't write at all,
And his heart was filled with yearnings for a certain Mr Hall;
Till, after many years of doubt, he sent his friend a card:
'Have tried to write an Algebra, but find it very hard.'

Now Mr Hall himself had tried to write a book for schools,
But suffered from a handicap: he didn't know the rules.
So when he heard from Mr Knight and understood his gist,
He answered him by telegram: 'Delighted to assist.'

So Mr Hall and Mr Knight they took a house together,
And they worked away at algebra in any kind of weather,
Determined not to give it up until they had evolved
A problem so constructed that it never could be solved.

'How hard it is,' said Mr Knight, 'to hide the fact from youth
That x and y are equal: it is such an obvious truth!'
'It is,' said Mr Hall, 'but if we gave a b to each,
We'd put the problem well beyond our little victims' reach.

'Or are you anxious, Mr Knight, lest any boy should see
The utter superfluity of this repeated b?'
'I scarcely fear it,' he replied, and scratched his grizzled head,
'But perhaps it *would* be safer if to b we added z.'

'A brilliant stroke!' said Hall, and added z to either side;
Then looked at his accomplice with a flush of happy pride.
And Knight, he winked at Hall (a very pardonable lapse),
And they printed off the Algebra and sold it to the chaps.

Eldorado

EDGAR ALLAN POE

Gaily bedight,
    A gallant knight,
In sunshine and in shadow,
    Had journeyed long,
    Singing a song,
In search of Eldorado.

But he grew old –
    This knight so bold –
And o'er his heart a shadow
    Fell as he found
    No spot of ground
That looked like Eldorado.

And, as his strength
    Failed him at length,
He met a pilgrim shadow:
    'Shadow,' said he,
    'Where can it be,
This land of Eldorado?'

'Over the mountains
    Of the Moon,
Down the valley of the Shadow,
    Ride, boldly ride,'
    The shade replied,
'If you seek for Eldorado.'

The Revenge, A Ballad of the Fleet

ALFRED LORD TENNYSON

At Flores in the Azores Sir Richard Grenville lay,
And a pinnace, like a flutter'd bird, came flying from far away:
'Spanish ships of war at sea! We have sighted fifty-three!'
Then sware Lord Thomas Howard: ' 'Fore God I am no coward;
But I cannot meet them here, for my ships are out of gear,
And the half my men are sick. I must fly, but follow quick.
We are six ships of the line; can we fight with fifty-three?'

Then spake Sir Richard Grenville: 'I know you are no coward;
You fly them for a moment to fight with them again.
But I've ninety men and more that are lying sick ashore.
I should count myself the coward if I left them, my Lord Howard,
To these Inquisition dogs and the devildoms of Spain.'

So Lord Howard passed away with five ships of war that day,
Till he melted like a cloud in the silent summer heaven;
But Sir Richard bore in hand all his sick men from the land
Very carefully and slow,
Men of Bideford in Devon,
And we laid them on the ballast down below;
For we brought them all aboard,
And they blessed him in their pain, that they were not left to Spain,
To the thumbscrew and the stake, for the glory of the Lord.

He had only a hundred seamen to work the ship and to fight,
And he sailed away from Flores till the Spaniard came in sight,
With his huge sea-castles heaving upon the weather bow.
'Shall we fight or shall we fly?
Good Sir Richard, tell us now,
For to fight is but to die!

87

There'll be little of us left by the time this sun be set.'
And Sir Richard said again: 'We be all good English men.
Let us bang these dogs of Seville, the children of the devil,
For I never turn'd my back upon Don or devil yet.'

Sir Richard spoke and he laugh'd, and we roared a hurrah, and so
The little Revenge ran on sheer into the heart of the foe,
With her hundred fighters on deck, and her ninety sick below;
For half of their fleet to the right and half to the left were seen,
And the little Revenge ran on thro' the long sea-lane between.

Thousands of their soldiers look'd down from their decks and laugh'd,
Thousands of their seamen made mock at the mad little craft
Running on and on, till delay'd
By their mountain-like San Philip that, of fifteen hundred tons,
And up-shadowing high above us with her yawning tiers of guns,
Took the breath from our sails, and we stay'd.

And while now the great San Philip hung above us like a cloud
Whence the thunderbolt will fall
Long and loud,
Four galleons drew away
From the Spanish fleet that day,
And two upon the larboard and two upon the starboard lay,
And the battle-thunder broke from them all.

But anon the great San Philip, she bethought herself and went
Having that within her womb that had left her ill content;
And the rest they came aboard us, and they fought us hand to hand,
For a dozen times they came with their pikes and musqueteers,
And a dozen times we shook 'em off as a dog that shakes his ears
When he leaps from the water to the land.

And the sun went down, and the stars came out far over the summer
    sea,
But never a moment ceased the fight of the one and the fifty-three.
Ship after ship, the whole night long, their high-built galleons came,
Ship after ship, the whole night long, with her battle-thunder and
    flame;
Ship after ship, the whole night long, drew back with her dead and
    her shame.
For some were sunk and many were shattered, and so could fight us
    no more –
God of battles, was ever a battle like this in the world before?

For he said 'Fight on! fight on!'
Though his vessel was all but a wreck;
And it chanc'd, that when half of the short summer night was gone,
With a grisly wound to be drest he had left the deck,
But a bullet struck him that was dressing it suddenly dead,
And himself he was wounded again in the side and the head,
And he said 'Fight on! fight on!'

And the night went down, and the sun smiled out far over the
    summer sea,
And the Spanish fleet with broken sides lay round us all in a ring;
But they dared not touch us again, for they fear'd that we still could
    sting,
So they watch'd what the end would be.
And we had not fought them in vain,
But in perilous plight were we,
Seeing forty of our poor hundred were slain,
And half of the rest of us maim'd for life
In the crash of the cannonades and the desperate strife;
And the sick men down in the hold were most of them stark and cold,
And the pikes were all broken or bent, and the powder was all of it
    spent;

And the masts and the rigging were lying over the side;
But Sir Richard cried in his English pride,
'We have fought such a fight for a day and a night
As may never be fought again!
We have won great glory, my men!
And a day less or more,
At sea or ashore,
We die – does it matter when?
Sink me the ship, Master Gunner, sink her, split her in twain!
Fall into the hands of God, not into the hands of Spain!'

And the gunner said 'Ay, ay,' but the seamen made reply:
'We have children, we have wives,
And the Lord hath spared our lives.
We will make the Spaniard promise, if we yield, to let us go;
We shall live to fight again and to strike another blow.'
And the lion there lay dying, and they yielded to the foe.

And the stately Spanish men to their flagship bore him then,
Where they laid him by the mast, old Sir Richard caught at last,
And they praised him to his face with their courtly foreign grace;
But he rose upon their decks and he cried:
'I have fought for Queen and Faith like a valiant man and true;
I have only done my duty as a man is bound to do:
With a joyful spirit I Sir Richard Grenville die!'
And he fell upon their decks, and he died.

And they stared at the dead that had been so valiant and true,
And had holden the power and glory of Spain so cheap
That he dared her with one little ship and his English few;
Was he devil or man? He was devil for aught they knew,
But they sank his body with honour down into the deep,
And they manned the Revenge with a swarthier, alien crew,
And away she sail'd with her loss and long'd for her own;
When a wind from the lands they had ruin'd awoke from sleep,

And the water began to heave and the weather to moan,
And or ever that evening ended a great gale blew,
And a wave like the wave that is raised by an earthquake grew,
Till it smote on their hulls and their sails and their masts and their
    flags,
And the whole sea plunged and fell on the shot-shatter'd navy of
    Spain,
And the little Revenge herself went down by the island crags
To be lost evermore in the main.

Lochinvar

SIR WALTER SCOTT

O, young Lochinvar has come out of the west,
Through all the wide Border, his steed was the best;
And save his good broadsword he weapons had none,
He rode all unarm'd and he rode all alone.
So faithful in love and so dauntless in war,
There never was knight like the young Lochinvar.

He staid not for brake, and he stopp'd not for stone,
He swam the Eske river where ford there was none;
But ere he alighted at Netherby gate,
The bride had consented; the gallant came late:
For a laggard in love and a dastard in war,
Was to wed the fair Ellen of brave Lochinvar.

So boldly he enter'd the Netherby Hall,
Among bride's-men and kinsmen and brothers and all:
Then spoke the bride's father, his hand on his sword,
(For the poor craven bridegroom said never a word):
'O come ye in peace here, or come ye in war,
Or to dance at our bridal, young Lord Lochinvar?'

'I long woo'd your daughter, my suit you denied;
Love swells like the Solway, but ebbs like its tide –
And now am I come, with this lost love of mine,
To lead but one measure, drink one cup of wine.
There are maidens in Scotland more lovely by far,
That would gladly be bride to the young Lochinvar.'

The bride kiss'd the goblet: the knight took it up,
He quaff'd off the wine, and he threw down the cup.
She look'd down to blush and she look'd up to sigh,
With a smile on her lips, and a tear in her eye.
  He took her soft hand ere her mother could bar,
  'Now tread me a measure!' said young Lochinvar.

So stately his form, and so lovely her face,
That never a hall such a galliard did grace;
While her mother did fret, and her father did fume,
And the bridegroom stood dangling his bonnet and plume;
  And the bride-maidens whispered, ' 'Twere better by far,
  To have matched our fair cousin with young Lochinvar.'

One touch to her hand, and one word in her ear,
When they reach'd the hall-door, and the charger stood near;
So light to the croupe the fair lady he swung,
So light to the saddle before her he sprung!
  'She is won! We are gone, over bank, bush and scaur;
  They'll have fleet steeds that follow!' quoth young Lochinvar.

There was mounting 'mong Graemes of the Netherby clan;
Forsters, Fenwicks and Musgraves, they rode and they ran:
There was racing and chasing, on Cannobie Lee,
But the lost bride of Netherby ne'er did they see.
  So daring in love, and so dauntless in war,
  Have ye e'er heard of gallant like young Lochinvar?

Thomas the Rhymer

ANONYMOUS

True Thomas lay on Huntlie bank;
    A ferlie he spied wi' his e'e;
And there he saw a ladye bright,
    Come riding down by the Eildon Tree.

Her skirt was o' the grass-green silk,
    Her mantle o' the velvet fine;
At ilka tett of her horse's mane,
    Hung fifty siller bells and nine.

True Thomas, he pull'd off his cap,
    And louted low down to his knee,
'All hail, thou mighty Queen of Heaven
    For thy peer on earth I never did see.'

'O no, O no, Thomas,' she said;
    'That name does not belong to me;
I am but the Queen of fair Elfland,
    That am hither come to visit thee.

'Harp and carp, Thomas,' she said;
    'Harp and carp along wi' me;
And if ye dare to kiss my lips,
    Sure of your bodie I will be.'

'Betide me weal, betide me woe,
    That weird shall never daunten me.'
Syne he has kiss'd her rosy lips,
    All underneath the Eildon Tree.

'Now, ye maun go wi' me,' she said;
    'True Thomas, ye maun go wi' me;
And ye maun serve me seven years,
    Thro' weal or woe as may chance to be.'

She mounted on her milk-white steed;
She's ta'en true Thomas up behind:
And aye, whene'er her bridle rung,
   The steed flew swifter than the wind.

O they rade on, and farther on;
   The steed gaed swifter than the wind;
Until they reached a desert wide,
   And living land was left behind.

'Light down, light down now, true Thomas,
   And lean your head upon my knee;
Abide and rest a little space,
   And I will shew you ferlies three.

'O see ye not yon narrow road,
   So thick beset with thorns and briers?
That is the path of righteousness,
   Though after it but few enquires.

'And see not ye that braid, braid road,
   That lies across that lily leven?
That is the path of wickedness,
   Though some call it the road to heaven.

'And see not ye that bonny road,
   That winds about the fernie brae?
That is the road to fair Elfland,
   Where thou and I this night maun gae.

'But, Thomas, ye maun hold your tongue
   Whatever ye may hear or see;
For, if ye speak word in Elfyn land,
   Ye'll ne'er get back to your ain countrie.'

O they rade on, and farther on,
  And they waded through rivers aboon the knee,
And they saw neither sun nor moon,
  But they heard the roaring of the sea.

It was mirk, mirk night, and there was nae star light,
  And they waded through red blude to the knee;
For a' the blude that's shed on earth
  Rins through the springs o' that countrie.

Syne they came to a garden green,
  And she pu'd an apple frae a tree:
'Take this for thy wages, true Thomas;
  It will give thee the tongue that can never lie.'

'My tongue is mine ain,' true Thomas said;
  'A gudely gift ye wad gie to me!
I neither dought to buy nor sell,
  At fair or tryst where I may be.

'I dought neither speak to prince or peer,
  Nor ask of grace from fair ladye.'
'Now hold thy peace!' the lady said,
  'For as I say, so must it be.'

He has gotten a coat of the even cloth,
  And a pair of shoes of velvet green;
And, till seven years were gane and past,
  True Thomas on earth was never seen.

The Bonny Earl of Moray

ANONYMOUS

Ye Hielands and ye Lawlands,
  Oh, where have you been?
They have slain the Earl of Moray,
  And have laid him on the green!

Oh wae betide thee, Huntly,
  And wherefore did you sae?
I bade you bring him wi' you,
  But forbade you him to slay.

He was a braw gallant,
  And he rade at the ring;
And the bonny Earl of Moray,
  He might have been a king!

He was a braw gallant,
  And he play'd at the ba';
And the bonny Earl of Moray,
  Was the flower amang them a'.

He was a braw gallant,
  And he play'd at the glove;
And the bonny Earl of Moray
  Oh he was the Queen's love!

Oh lang, lang will his lady
  Look frae the Castle Doune,
Ere she see the Earl of Moray
  Come sounding thro' the town!

Ye Hielands and ye Lawlands,
  Oh, where have you been?
They have slain the Earl of Moray,
  And have laid him on the green!

The Twa Corbies

ANONYMOUS

As I was walking all alane,
I heard twa corbies making a mane;
The tane unto the t'other did say,
'Where sall we gang and dine to-day?'

'In behint yon auld fail dyke,
I wot there lies a new-slain knight;
And nae body kens that he lies there,
But his hawk, his hound and his lady fair.

'His hound is to the hunting gane,
His hawk to fetch the wild-fowl hame,
His lady's ta'en another mate,
So we may make our dinner sweet.

'Ye'll sit on his white hause bane,
And I'll pike out his bonny blue e'en:
Wi' ae lock o' his gowden hair,
We'll theek our nest when it grows bare.

'Mony a one for him makes mane,
But nane sall ken whare he is gane:
O'er his white banes, when they are bare,
The wind sall blaw for evermair.'

Sir Patrick Spens

ANONYMOUS

The king sits in Dunfermline town,
   Drinking the blude-red wine;
'O where will I get a skeely skipper,
   To sail this new ship of mine!'

O up and spake an eldern knight,
   Sat at the king's right knee –
'Sir Patrick Spens is the best sailor
   That ever sail'd the sea.'

Our king has written a braid letter,
   And seal'd it with his hand,
And sent it to Sir Patrick Spens,
   Was walking on the strand.

'To Noroway, to Noroway,
   To Noroway o'er the faem:
The king's daughter of Noroway,
   'Tis thou maun bring her hame.'

The first word that Sir Patrick read,
   Sae loud, loud laughed he;
The neist word that Sir Patrick read,
   The tear blinded his e'e.

'O wha is this has done this deed,
   And tauld the king o' me,
To send us out, at this time of the year,
   To sail upon the sea?

'Be it wind, be it weet, be it hail, be it sleet,
   Our ship must sail the faem;
The king's daughter of Noroway,
   'Tis we must fetch her hame.'

They hoysted their sails on Monenday morn,
   Wi' a' the speed they may;
They hae landed in Noroway,
   Upon a Wodensday.

They hadna been a week, a week,
   In Noroway, but twae,
When that the lords o' Noroway
   Began aloud to say –

'Ye Scottishmen spend a' our king's goud,
   And a' our queenis fee.'
'Ye lie, ye lie, ye liars loud!
   Fu' loud I hear ye lie.

'For I brought as much white monie,
   As gane my men and me,
And I brought a half-fou o' gude red goud,
   Out o'er the sea wi' me.

'Make ready, make ready, my merry men a'!
   Our gade ship sails the morn.'
'Now, ever alake, my master dear,
   I fear a deadly storm!'

'I saw the new moon, late yestreen,
   Wi' the auld moon in her arm;
And if we gang to sea, master,
   I fear we'll come to harm.'

They hadna sail'd a league, a league,
　　A league but barely three,
When the lift grew dark, and the wind blew loud,
　　And gurly grew the sea.

The ankers brak, and the topmasts lap,
　　It was sic a deadly storm;
And the waves cam' o'er the broken ship,
　　Till a' her sides were torn.

'O where will I get a gude sailor,
　　To take my helm in hand,
Till I get up to the tall top-mast,
　　To see if I can spy land?'

'O here am I, a sailor gude,
　　To take the helm in hand,
Till you go up to the tall top-mast;
　　But I fear you'll ne'er spy land.'

He hadna gane a step, a step,
　　A step but barely ane,
When a bout flew out of our goodly ship,
　　And the salt sea it came in.

'Gae fetch a web o' the silken claith,
　　Another o' the twine,
And wap them into our ship's side,
　　And let na the sea come in.'

They fetched a web o' the silken claith,
　　Another o' the twine,
And they wapped them round that gude ship's side,
　　But still the sea came in.

O laith, laith, were our gude Scots lords
　　To weet their cork-heel'd shoon!
But lang or a' the play was play'd,
　　They wat their hats aboon.

And mony was the feather-bed
　　That flatter'd on the faem;
And mony was the gude lord's son
　　That never mair cam hame.

The ladyes wrang their fingers white,
　　The maidens tore their hair,
A' for the sake of their true loves;
　　For them they'll see nae mair.

O lang, lang, may the ladyes sit,
　　Wi' their fans into their hand,
Before they see Sir Patrick Spens
　　Come sailing to the strand!

And lang, lang, may the maidens sit,
　　Wi' their goud kaims in their hair,
A' waiting for their ain dear loves!
　　For them they'll see na mair.

Half-owre, half-owre to Aberdour,
　　'Tis fifty fathoms deep,
And there lies gude Sir Patrick Spens,
　　Wi' the Scots lords at his feet!

King John and the Abbot of Canterbury

ANONYMOUS

An ancient story I'll tell you anon,
Of a notable prince that was called King John;
And he ruled over England with main and might,
But he did great wrong, and maintained little right.

And I'll tell you a story, a story so merry,
Concerning the Abbot of Canterbury;
How for his housekeeping and high renown,
They rode post for him to fair London town.

A hundred men, the King did hear say,
The Abbot kept in his house every day;
And fifty gold chains, without any doubt,
In velvet coats waited the Abbot about.

'How now, Father Abbot! I hear it of thee,
Thou keepest a far better house than me;
And for thy housekeeping and high renown,
I fear thou work'st treason against my crown.'

'My Liege,' quoth the Abbot. 'I would it were known,
I never spend nothing but what is my own;
And I trust your grace will do me no deere
For spending my own true gotten geare.'

'Yes, yes, Father Abbot, thy fault it is high,
And now for the same thou needest must die;
For except thou canst answer my questions three,
Thy head shall be smitten from thy bodie.

'And first,' quoth the King, 'when I'm in this stead,
With my crown of gold so fair on my head,
Among all my liege-men so noble of birth,
Thou must tell me to one penny what I am worth.

'Secondly tell me, without any doubt,
How soon I may ride the whole world about;
And at the third question thou must not shrink,
But tell me here truly what I do think.'

'O these are hard questions for my shallow wit,
Nor I cannot answer your grace as yet;
But if you will give me but three weeks' space,
I'll do my endeavour to answer your grace.'

'Now three weeks' space to thee will I give,
And that is the longest time thou hast to live;
For if thou dost not answer my questions three,
Thy life and thy living are forfeit to me.'

Away rode the Abbot, all sad at that word,
And he rode to Cambridge and Oxenford;
But never a doctor there was so wise,
That could with his learning an answer devise.

Then home rode the Abbot of comfort so cold,
And he met his shepherd a-going to fold;
'How now, my lord Abbot, you are welcome home:
What news do you bring us from good King John?'

'Sad news, sad news, Shepherd, I must give;
That I have but three days more to live.
For if I do not answer him questions three,
My head will be smitten from my bodie.

'The first is to tell him there in that stead,
With his crown of gold so fair on his head,
Among all his liege-men so noble of birth,
To within one penny, of what he is worth.

'The second, to tell him, without any doubt,
How soon he may ride this whole world about;
And at the third question I must not shrink,
But tell him there truly, what he does think.'

'Now cheer up, Sir Abbot, did you never hear yet
That a fool he may learn a wise man wit!
Lend me horse and serving men and your apparel,
And I'll ride to London to answer your quarrel.

'Nay frown not, if it hath been told unto me,
I am like your lordship as ever may be;
And if you will but lend me your gown,
There is none shall know us in fair London town.'

'Now horses and serving-men thou shalt have,
With sumptuous array most gallant and brave,
With crozier and mitre and rochet and cope,
Fit to appear 'fore our father, the Pope.'

'Now welcome, Sir Abbot,' the King he did say,
' 'Tis well thou'rt come back to keep thy day;
For and if thou canst answer my questions three,
Thy life and thy living, both saved shall be.

'And first, when thou seest me here in this stead,
With my crown of gold so fair on my head,
Among all my liege-men so noble of birth,
Tell me to one penny what I am worth.'

'For thirty pence our Saviour was sold
Among the false Jews, as I have been told:
And twenty-nine is the worth of thee,
For I think thou art one penny worser than He.'

The King he laughed, and swore by St Bittel,
'I did not think I had been worth so little!
Now secondly tell me, without any doubt,
How soon I may ride this whole world about.'

'You must rise with the sun, and ride with the same,
Until the next morning he riseth again;
And then your Grace need not make any doubt
But in twenty-four hours, you'll ride it about.'

The King he laughed, and swore by St Jone,
'I did not think it could be done so soon.
Now from the third question thou must not shrink,
But tell me here truly what I do think.'

'Yea, that I shall do, and make your Grace merry!
You think I'm the Abbot of Canterbury.
But I'm his poor shepherd, as plain you may see,
That am come to beg pardon for him and for me.'

The King he laughed, and swore by the Mass,
'I'll make thee Lord Abbot this day in his place!'
'Nay, nay, my Liege, be not in such speed,
For alack, I can neither write nor read.'

'Four nobles a week then, I will give thee;
For this merry jest thou hast shown unto me.
And tell the old Abbot, when thou comest home,
Thou hast brought him a pardon from good King John.'

La Belle Dame Sans Merci

JOHN KEATS

O what can ail thee Knight at arms,
  Alone and palely loitering?
The sedge has withered from the Lake,
  And no birds sing!

O what can ail thee Knight at arms,
  So haggard, and so woe begone?
The Squirrel's granary is full
  And the harvest's done.

I see a lilly on thy brow
  With anguish moist and fever dew,
And on thy cheeks a fading rose
  Fast withereth too.

I met a Lady in the meads
  Full beautiful, a faery's child,
Her hair was long, her foot was light,
  And her eyes were wild.

I made a Garland for her head,
  And bracelets too, and fragrant Zone;
She look'd at me as she did love
  And made sweet moan.

I set her on my pacing steed
  And nothing else saw all day long;
For sidelong would she bend and sing
  A faery's song.

She found me roots of relish sweet
   And honey wild and manna dew;
And sure in language strange she said —
   I love thee true.

She took me to her elfin grot,
   And there she wept and sigh'd full sore;
And there I shut her wild wild eyes
   With kisses four.

And there she lulled me asleep,
   And there I dream'd, Ah Woe betide!
The latest dream I ever dreamt
   On the cold hill side.

I saw pale Kings, and Princes too,
   Pale warriors, death pale were they all;
They cried, 'La Belle Dame sans Merci
   Thee hath in thrall!'

I saw their starv'd lips in the gloam
   With horrid warning gaped wide,
And I awoke, and found me here
   On the cold hill's side.

And this is why I sojourn here
   Alone and palely loitering,
Though the sedge is withered from the Lake,
   And no birds sing.

The Secret

ANONYMOUS

O hame came our good man at e'en, and hame came he,
And there he saw a horse hitched where no horse should be.
  'Wife,' quo' he, 'How can this be?
  How came this horse here wi'out the leave o' me?'
     'Horse?' quo' she.
     'Aye, horse,' quo' he.
  'Ye auld blin' donnert carl, and blin'er mought you be,
   That's but a fine new milch cow my minnie brought to me.'
'Far hae I travelled and muckle hae I seen,
But saddles upon milch cows, saw I never nane.'

O hame came our good man at e'en, and hame came he,
And there he saw a riding whip where no whip should be.
  'Wife,' quo' he, 'How can this be?
  How came this Whip here wi'out the leave o' me?'
     ' Whip?' quo' she.
     'Aye, whip,' quo' he.
  'Ye auld blin' donnert carl, and blin'er mought you be,
   That's but a fine new porridge stick my minnie brought to me.'
'Far hae I travelled and muckle hae I seen,
But tassels upon porridge sticks, saw I never nane.'

O hame came our good man at e'en, and hame came he,
And there he saw fine riding boots where no boots should be.
  'Wife,' quo' he, 'How can this be?
  How came these boots here wi'out the leave o' me?'
     'Boots?' quo' she.
     'Aye, boots,' quo' he.
  'Ye auld blin' donnert carl, and blin'er mought you be,
   That's but a pair of milking stoups my minnie brought to me.

'Far hae I travelled and muckle hae I seen,
But spurs on milking stoups, saw I never nane.'

O hame came our good man at e'en, and hame came he,
And there he saw a man asleep where no man should be.
  'Wife,' quo' he, 'How can this be?
  You're hiding *Chairlie* i' the house, wi'out the leave o' me!'

The Leech Gatherer

WILLIAM WORDSWORTH

There was a roaring in the wind all night;
    The rain came heavily and fell in floods;
But now the sun is rising calm and bright.
    The birds are singing in the distant woods;
    Over his own sweet voice the Stock-dove broods.
The Jay makes answer as the Magpie chatters;
And all the air is filled with pleasant noise of waters.

All things that love the sun are out of doors;
    The sky rejoices in the morning's birth;
The grass is bright with rain-drops. On the moors
    The hare is running races in her mirth;
    And with her feet she from the plashy earth
Raises a mist that, glittering in the sun,
Runs with her all the way, wherever she doth run.

I heard the sky-lark warbling in the sky,
    And I bethought me of the playful hare:
Even such a happy Child of earth am I;
    Even as these blissful creatures do I fare;
    Far from the world I walk, and from all care;
But there may come another day to me –
Solitude, pain of heart, distress, and poverty.

Now, whether it were by peculiar grace,
    A leading from above, a something given,
Yet it befell that, in this lonely place,
    When I with these untoward thoughts had striven,
    Beside a pool bare to the eye of heaven
I saw a Man before me unawares:
The oldest man he seemed that ever wore grey hairs.

Himself he propped, limbs, body, and pale face,
　　Upon a long grey staff of shaven wood:
And, still as I drew near with gentle pace,
　　Upon the margin of that moorish flood
　　Motionless as a cloud the old Man stood,
That heareth not the loud winds when they call;
And moveth all together, if it move at all.

At length, himself unsettling, he the pond
　　Stirred with his staff, and fixedly did look
Upon the muddy water, which he conned,
　　As if he had been reading in a book.
　　And now a stranger's privilege I took:
And, drawing to his side, to him did say:
'This morning gives us promise of a glorious day.'

A gentle answer did the old Man make,
　　In courteous speech which forth he slowly drew:
And him with further words I thus bespake:
　　'What occupation do you there pursue?
　　This is a lonesome place for one like you.'
Ere he replied, a flash of mild surprise
Broke from the sable orbs of his yet-vivid eyes.

He told, that to these waters he had come
　　To gather leeches, being old and poor –
Employment hazardous and wearisome!
　　And he had many hardships to endure:
　　From pond to pond he roamed, from moor to moor;
Housing, with God's good help, by choice or chance;
And in this way he gained an honest maintenance.

My former thoughts returned; the fear that kills;
　　And hope that is unwilling to be fed;
Cold, pain, and labour, and all fleshly ills;
　　And mighty Poets in their misery dead.
　　Perplexed, and longing to be comforted,
My question eagerly did I renew,
'How is it that you live, and what is it you do?'

He with a smile did then his words repeat;
　　And said that, gathering leeches, far and wide
He travelled; stirring thus about his feet
　　The waters of the pools where they abide.
　　'Once I could meet with them on every side;
But they have dwindled long by slow decay;
Yet still I persevere, and find them where I may.'

And soon with this he other matter blended,
　　Cheerfully uttered, with demeanour kind,
But stately in the main; and when he ended,
　　I could have laughed myself to scorn to find
　　In that decrepit Man so firm a mind.
'God,' said I, 'be my help and stay secure;
I'll think of the Leech-gatherer on the lonely moor!'

Token of All Brave Captains

CAPTAIN MARRYAT

The captain stood on the carronade: 'First Lieutenant,' says he,
'Send all my merry men aft here, for they must list to me.
I haven't the gift of the gab, my sons – because I'm bred to the sea;
That ship there is a Frenchman, who means to fight with we.
   And odds bobs, hammer and tongs, long as I've been to sea,
   I've fought 'gainst every odds – but I've gained the victory!

'That ship there is a Frenchman, and if we don't take she,
'Tis a thousand bullets to one, that she will capture we.
I haven't the gift of the gab, my boys, so each man to his gun;
If she's not mine in half an hour, I'll flog each mother's son.
   For odds bobs, hammer and tongs, long as I've been to sea,
   I've fought 'gainst every odds – and I've gained the victory!'

We fought for twenty minutes, when the Frenchman had enough;
'I little thought,' said he, 'that your men were of such stuff.'
Our captain took the Frenchman's sword, a low bow made to he;
'I haven't the gift of the gab, monsieur, but polite I wish to be.
   And odds bobs, hammer and tongs, long as I've been to sea,
   I've fought 'gainst every odds – and I've gained the victory!'

Our captain sent for all of us: 'My merry men,' said he,
'I haven't the gift of the gab, my lads, but yet I thankful be:
You've done your duty handsomely, each man stood to his gun;
If you hadn't, you villains, sure as day, I'd have flogged each mother's
   son,
   For odds bobs, hammer and tongs, as long as I'm at sea,
   I'll fight 'gainst every odds – and I'll gain the victory!'

Little Billee

WILLIAM MAKEPEACE THACKERAY

There were three sailors of Bristol city
   Who took a boat and went to sea.
But first with beef and captain's biscuits
   And pickled pork they loaded she.

There was gorging Jack and guzzling Jimmy,
   And the youngest he was little Billee.
Now when they got as far as the Equator
   They'd nothing left but one split pea.

Says gorging Jack to guzzling Jimmy,
   'I am extremely hungaree.'
To gorging Jack says guzzling Jimmy,
   'We've nothing left, us must eat we.'

Says gorging Jack to guzzling Jimmy,
   'With one another we shouldn't agree!
There's little Bill, he's young and tender,
   We're old and tough, so let's eat he.

'Oh! Billy, we're going to kill and eat you,
   So undo the button of your chemie.'
When Bill received this information
   He used his pocket handkerchie.

'First let me say my catechism,
   Which my poor mammy taught to me.'
'Make haste, make haste,' says guzzling Jimmy,
   While Jack pulled out his snickersnee.

So Billy went up to the main-top gallant mast,
    And down he fell on his bended knee.
He scarce had come to the twelfth commandment
    When up he jumps. 'There's land I see:

'Jerusalem and Madagascar,
    And North and South Amerikee:
There's the British flag a riding at anchor,
    With Admiral Napier, K.C.B.'

So when they got aboard of the Admiral's
    He hanged fat Jack and flogged Jimmee:
But as for little Bill, he made him
    The Captain of a Seventy-three.

The Raiders

WILL H. OGILVIE

Last night a wind from Lammermoor came roaring up the glen
With the tramp of trooping horses and the laugh of reckless men
And struck a mailed hand on the gate and cried in rebel glee:
  'Come forth! Come forth, my Borderer, and ride the March
    with me!'

I said, 'O Wind of Lammermoor, the night's too dark to ride,
And all the men that fill the glen are ghosts of men that died!
The floods are down in Bowmont Burn, the moss is fetlock deep.
  Go back, wild Wind of Lammermoor to Lauderdale and sleep!'

Out spoke the Wind of Lammermoor, 'We know the road right well,
The road that runs by Kale and Jed across the Carter Fell.
There is no man of all the men in this bold troop of mine
  But blind might ride the Borderside from Teviothead to Tyne!'

The horses fretted on their bits and pawed the flints to fire,
The riders swung to saddle facing South to their desire;
'Come!' said the Wind from Lammermoor, and spoke right scorn-
    fully,
  'Have ye no pride to mount and ride your grandsire's road with
    me?'

A roan horse to the gate they led, foam-flecked and travelled far,
A snorting roan that tossed his head and flashed his forehead star;
There came a sound of clashing steel and hoof-tramp up the glen,
  And two by two we cantered through, a troop of ghostly men!

* * *

I know not if the farms we fired are burned to ashes yet!
I know not if the stirks grew tired before the stars had set!
I only know that late last night when northern winds blew free
  A troop of men rode up the glen and brought a horse for me!

4 · HOMELY THINGS

—

My Mother Said

ANONYMOUS

My mother said, I never should
Play with gypsies in the wood.

If I did, then she would say:
'Naughty girl to disobey!

'Your hair shan't curl and your shoes shan't shine,
You gypsy girl, you shan't be mine!'

And my father said that if I did,
He'd rap my head with the teapot-lid.

My mother said that I never should
Play with the gypsies in the wood.

The wood was dark, the grass was green;
By came Sally with a tambourine.

I went to sea – no ship to get across;
I paid ten shillings for a blind white horse.

I upped on his back and was off in a crack,
Sally tell my mother I shall never come back.

There was a Naughty Boy

JOHN KEATS

There was a naughty boy,
And a naughty boy was he.
He ran away to Scotland,
The people for to see.
Then he found
That the ground
Was as hard,
That a yard
Was as long,
That a song
Was as merry,
That a cherry
Was as red,
That lead
Was as weighty,
That four-score
Was as eighty,
And a door
Was as wooden
As in England.
So he stood in his shoes,
And he wondered,
He wondered,
He stood in his shoes
And he wondered.

He that Spendeth Much

HUGH RHODES

He that spendeth much;
    And getteth nought;
He that oweth much,
    And hath nought;
He that looketh in his purse
    And findeth nought –
He may be sorry;
    And say nought.

He that may and will not,
He then that would, shall not,
He that would, and cannot,
May repent and sigh not.

He that sweareth
    Till no man trust him;
He that lieth
    Till no man believe him;
He that borroweth
    Till no man will lend him;
Let him go where
    No man knoweth him.

He that hath a good master,
    And cannot keep him;
He that hath a good servant,
    And is not content with him;
He that hath such conditions,
    That no man loveth him;
May well know other,
    But few men will know him.

Up at a Villa – Down in the City

ROBERT BROWNING

Had I but plenty of money,
    money enough and to spare,
The house for me, no doubt,
    were a house in the city square:
Ah, such a life, such a life,
    as one leads at the window there!

Something to see, by Bacchus,
    something to hear, at least!
There, the whole day long,
    one's life is a perfect feast;
While up at a villa one lives,
    I maintain it, no more than a beast.

But bless you, it's dear – it's dear!
    fowls, wine, at double the rate.
They have clapped a new tax upon salt,
    and what oil pays, passing the gate –
It's a horror to think of.
    And so, the villa for me, not the city!
Beggars can scarcely be choosers:
    but still – ah, the pity, the pity.

Deeds not Words

ANONYMOUS

A man of words and not of deeds
Is like a garden full of weeds;

And when the weeds begin to grow,
It's like a garden full of snow;

And when the snow begins to fall,
It is like birds upon a wall;

And when the birds begin to fly,
It's like a shipwreck in the sky;

And when the sky begins to roar,
It's like a lion at the door;

And when the door begins to crack,
It's like a stick across your back;

And when your back begins to smart,
It's like a penknife in your heart;

And when your heart begins to bleed,
Oh then you're dead and dead indeed!

A Thanksgiving to God for his House

ROBERT HERRICK

Lord, Thou hast given me a cell
    Wherein to dwell;
A little house, whose humble roof
    Is weather-proof;
Under the spars of which I lie
    Both soft and dry;
Where Thou my chamber for to ward
    Hast set a Guard
Of harmless thoughts, to watch and keep
    Me, while I sleep.

Low is my porch, as is my Fate,
    Both void of state;
And yet the threshold of my door
    Is worn by the poor,
Who hither come, and freely get
    Good words, or meat:

Like as my parlour, so my hall
    And kitchen's small:
A little buttery, and therein
    A little bin,
Which keeps my little loaf of bread
    Unchipped, unflead.

Some brittle sticks of thorn or briar
    Make me a fire,
Close by whose living coal I sit,
    And glow like it.

Lord, I confess too, when I dine,
    The pulse is thine,
And all those other bits that be
    There placed by Thee;
The worts, the purslain, and the messe
    Of watercress,
Which of Thy kindness Thou hast sent;
    And my content
Makes those and my beloved beet,
    To be more sweet.

'Tis Thou that crown'st my glittering hearth
    With guiltless mirth;
And giv'st me wassail bowls to drink,
    Spiced to the brink.
Lord, 'tis thy plenty-dropping hand,
    That soils my land,
And giv'st me, for my bushel sown,
    Twice ten for one.

Thou mak'st my teaming hen to lay
    Her egg each day:
Besides, my healthful ewes to bear
    Me twins each year:
The while the conduits of my kine
    Run cream (for wine).

All these and better Thou dost send
    Me, to this end,
That I should render, for my part,
    A thankful heart;
Which, fir'd with incense, I resign
    As wholly thine;
But the acceptance, that must be,
    My Christ, by Thee.

Winter

WILLIAM SHAKESPEARE

When icicles hang by the wall,
  And Dick the shepherd blows his nail,
And Tom bears logs into the hall,
  And milk comes frozen home in pail;
When blood is nipp'd and ways be foul,
Then nightly sings the staring owl,
      To-whit! to-who!
      A merry note,
While greasy Joan doth keel the pot.

When all aloud the wind doth blow,
  And coughing drowns the parson's saw;
And birds sit brooding in the snow,
  And Marian's nose looks red and raw;
When roasted crabs hiss in the bowl,
Then nightly sings the staring owl,
      To-whit! to-who!
      A merry note,
While greasy Joan doth keel the pot.

God be in my Head

ANONYMOUS

God be in my head
And in my Understanding.

God be in my eyes
And in my Looking.

God be in my mouth
And in my Speaking.

God be in my heart
And in my Thinking.

God be at mine end
And at my Departing.

Let Dogs Delight

ISAAC WATTS

Let dogs delight to bark and bite,
    For God hath made them so;
Let bears and lions growl and fight
    For 'tis their nature too.

But children, you should never let
    Your angry passions rise;
Your little hands were never made
    To tear each other's eyes.

Let love through all your actions run,
    And all your words be mild;
Live like the Blessed Virgin's Son,
    That sweet and lovely child.

Dont-Care

ANONYMOUS

Dont-care didn't care;
　Dont-care was wild.
Dont-care stole plum and pear
　Like any beggar's child.

Dont-care was made to care,
　Dont-care was hung:
Dont-care was put in the pot
　And boiled till he was done.

A Farewell

CHARLES KINGSLEY

My fairest child, I have no song to give you;
　No lark could pipe in skies so dull and grey;
Yet, if you will, one quiet hint I'll leave you,
　For every day.

I'll tell you how to sing a clearer carol
　Than lark who hails the dawn on breezy down;
To earn yourself a purer poet's laurel
　Than Shakespeare's crown.

Be good, sweet maid, and let who can be clever;
　Do noble things, not dream them, all day long;
And so make Life, Death and that last For Ever,
　One grand sweet song.

Sweet Neglect

BEN JONSON

Still to be neat, still to be drest,
As you were going to a feast:
Still to be powder'd, still perfumed:
Lady, it is to be presumed,
Though art's hid causes are not found,
All is not sweet, all is not sound.

Give me a look, give me a face
That makes simplicity a grace;
Robes loosely flowing, hair as free:
Such sweet neglect more taketh me,
Than all th'adulteries of art
That strike mine eyes, but not my heart.

Loving and Liking

DOROTHY WORDSWORTH

There's more in words than I can teach:
Yet listen, Child – I would not preach,
But only give some plain directions
To guide your speech and your affections.

Say not you LOVE a roasted fowl,
But you may love a screaming owl
And, if you can, the unwieldy toad
That crawls from his secure abode
Within the mossy garden wall
When evening dews begin to fall.

And when, upon some showery day,
Into a path or public way
A frog leaps out from bordering grass,
Startling the timid as they pass,
Do you observe him, and endeavour
To take the intruder into favour;
Learning from him to find a reason
For a light heart in a dull season.

The spring's first rose by you espied
May fill your breast with joyful pride;
And you may love the strawberry-flower,
And love the strawberry in its bower;
But when the fruit, so often praised
For beauty, to your lip is raised,
Say not you LOVE the delicate treat,
But LIKE it, enjoy it, and thankfully eat.

Long may you love your pensioner mouse,
Though one of a tribe that torment the house:
Nor dislike her cruel sport the cat,
Deadly foe both of mouse and rat.

Remember she follows the law of her kind,
And Instinct is neither wayward nor blind.
Then think of her beautiful gliding form,
Her tread that would scarcely crush a worm,
And her soothing song by the winter fire,
Soft as the dying throb of the lyre.

I would not circumscribe your love:
It may soar with the eagle and brood with the dove,
May pierce the earth with the patient mole,
Or track the hedgehog to his hole.
Loving and liking are the solace of life,
Rock the cradle of joy, smooth the death-bed of strife.

You love your father and your mother,
Your grown-up and your baby brother;
You love your sister, and your friends,
And countless blessings, which God sends:
But LIKINGS come, and pass away;
'Tis love that remains till our latest day.

Domestic Economy

ANNA WICKHAM

I will have few cooking-pots,
They shall be bright;
They shall reflect to blinding
God's straight light.
I will have four garments,
They shall be clean;
My service shall be good,
Though my diet be mean,
Then I shall have excess to give to the poor,
And right to counsel beggars at my door.

Sweet are the Thoughts

ROBERT GREENE

Sweet are the thoughts that savour of content:
　　The quiet mind is richer than a crown.
Sweet are the nights in careless slumber spent;
　　The poor estate scorns fortune's angry frown.
Such sweet content, such minds, such sleep, such bliss
　　Beggars enjoy when princes oft do miss.

The homely house that harbours quiet rest,
　　The cottage that affords no pride nor care,
The mean that 'grees with country music best,
　　The sweet consort of mirth and music's fare,
Obscured life sets down a type of bliss:
　　A mind content, both crown and kingdom is.

An Old Woman of the Roads

PADRAIC COLUM

O, to have a little house!
  To own the hearth and stool and all!
The heap'd-up sods upon the fire,
  The pile of turf against the wall!

To have a clock with weights and chains
  And pendulum swinging up and down!
A dresser filled with shining delph,
  Speckled and white and blue and brown!

I could be busy all the day
  Clearing and sweeping hearth and floor;
And fixing on their shelf again
  My white and blue and speckled store!

I could be quiet there at night
  Beside the fire and by myself,
Sure of a bed and loth to leave
  The ticking and the shining delph!

Och! but I'm weary of mist and dark,
  And roads where there's never a house nor bush,
And tired I am of bog and road,
  And the crying wind and the lonesome hush!

And I am praying to God on high,
  And I am praying Him night and day,
For a little house – a house of my own –
  Out of the wind's and the rain's way.

Greedy Richard

JANE TAYLOR

'I think I want some pies this morning,'
Said Dick, stretching himself and yawning
So down he threw his slate and books,
And sauntered to the pastry cook's.

And there he cast his greedy eyes
Round on the jellies and the pies,
So to select with anxious care
The very nicest that was there.

At last the point was well decided –
As his opinion was divided
'Twixt pie and jelly, being loth
Either to leave – he took them both.

Now Richard never could be pleased
To stop when hunger was appeased;
But would go on to eat still more
Though he had had an ample store.

'No, not another now,' said Dick,
'Dear me! I feel extremely sick.
I cannot even eat this bit.
I wish – I – had not – tasted – it.'

Then slowly rising from his seat
He threw his cheesecake in the street,
And left the tempting pastry-cook's
With very discontented looks.

Bed in Summer

ROBERT LOUIS STEVENSON

In winter I get up at night
And dress by yellow candle-light.
In summer, quite the other way,
I have to go to bed by day.

I have to go to bed and see
The birds still hopping on the tree,
Or hear the grown-up people's feet
Still going past me in the street.

And does it not seem hard to you,
When all the sky is clear and blue,
And I should like so much to play,
To have to go to bed by day?

Charles Augustus Fortescue

who always did what was right, and so accumulated an immense fortune

HILAIRE BELLOC

The nicest child I ever knew
Was Charles Augustus Fortescue.
He never lost his cap, or tore
His stockings or his pinafore:
In eating Bread he made no Crumbs;
He was extremely fond of Sums,
To which, however, he preferred
The Parsing of a Latin Word –
He sought, when it was in his power,
For information twice an hour,
And as for finding Mutton-Fat
Unappetising, far from that!
He often, at his Father's Board,
Would beg them, of his own accord,
To give him if they did not mind,
The Greasiest Morsels they could find –
His Later Years did not belie
The Promise of his Infancy.
In Public Life he always tried
To take a judgement Broad and Wide;
In Private, none was more than he
Renowned for quiet courtesy.
He rose at once in his Career,
And long before his Fortieth Year,
Had wedded Fifi, Only Child
Of Bunyan, First Lord Alberfylde.
He thus became immensely Rich
And built the Splendid Mansion which

Is called The Cedars, Muswell Hill,
Where he resides in Affluence still,
To show what Everybody might
Become by
  SIMPLY DOING RIGHT.

Poverty

THOMAS TRAHERNE

As in the house I sate
Alone and desolate,
No creature but the fire and I,
The chimney and the stool, I lift mine eye
Up to the wall,
And in the silent hall
Saw nothing mine
But some few cups and dishes shine,
The table and the wooden stools
Where people used to dine:
A painted cloth there was
Wherein some ancient story wrought
A little entertain'd my thought
Which light discover'd through the glass.

I wonder'd much to see
That all my wealth should be
Confin'd in such a little room,
Yet hope for more I scarcely durst presume.
It griev'd me sore
That such a scanty store
Should be my all:
For I forgot my ease and health,
Nor did I think of hands or eyes,
Nor soul nor body prize;
I neither thought the sun,
Nor moon, nor stars, nor people, *mine*,
Though they did round about me shine;
And therefore was I quite undone.

Some greater things I thought
　　Must needs for me be wrought,
Which till my craving mind could see
I ever should lament my poverty:
　　　I fain would have
　　Whatever bounty gave;
　　　Nor could there be
Without, or love or deity:
For, should not he be infinite
　　Whose hand created me?
　　Ten thousand absent things
Did vex my poor and wanting mind,
Which, till I be no longer blind,
Let me not see the King of Kings.

Corn-riggs are Bonny

ANONYMOUS

There was a piper had a cow
　　And had no hay to give her.
He played a tune upon his pipes,
　　'Consider, old cow, consider!'

The old cow considered well
　　And promised her master money,
Only to play that other tune,
　　'Corn-riggs are bonny.'

Whole Duty of Children

ROBERT LOUIS STEVENSON

A child should always say what's true,
And speak when he is spoken to,
And behave mannerly at table:
At least as far as he is able.

Sing a Song of Honey

BARBARA EUPHAN TODD

Honey from the white rose, honey from the red,
Is not that a pretty thing to spread upon your bread?
When the flower is open, the bee begins to buzz,
I'm very glad, I'm very glad, I'm very glad it does –
Honey from the lily,
   Honey from the May,
AND the daffodilly,
   AND the lilac spray –
When the snow is falling, when the fires are red,
Is not that a pretty thing to spread upon your bread?

Honey from the heather, honey from the lime,
Is not that a dainty thing to eat in winter-time?
Honey from the cherry, honey from the ling,
Honey from the celandine that opens in the Spring.
Honey from the clover,
   Honey from the pear –
Summer may be over,
   But I shall never care.
When the fires are blazing, honey from the lime
Makes a very dainty dish to eat in winter-time.

Kings will leave their counting any time they're told
Queens are in the parlour spreading honey gold,
Gold from honeysuckle, gold from lupins' spire –
Who will stay in counting-house and miss the parlour fire?
Honey from the daisy,
   Honey from the plum,
Kings will all be lazy,
   And glad that Winter's come.
Who will keep to counting till the sum is told?
I'll be in the parlour and eating honey-gold.

The Waggoner

WILLIAM WORDSWORTH

'Tis spent – this burning day of June!
Soft darkness o'er its latest gleams is stealing;
The buzzing dor-hawk, round and round, is wheeling –
    That solitary bird
    Is all that can be heard
In silence deeper far than that of deepest noon!

Hush, there is someone on the stir!
'Tis Benjamin the Waggoner,
Who long hath trod this toilsome way,
Companion of the night and day.
That far-off tinkling's drowsy cheer,
Mix'd with a faint yet grating sound
In a moment lost and found,
The Wain announces – by whose side
Along the banks of Rydal Mere
He paces on, a trusty Guide –
Listen! you can scarcely hear!
Hither he his course is bending;
Now he leaves the lower ground,
And up the craggy hill ascending
Many a stop and stay he makes,
Many a breathing-fit he takes;
Steep the way and wearisome,
Yet all the while his whip is dumb!

The Horses have worked with right goodwill,
And so have gained the top of the hill.
He was patient, they were strong,
And now they smoothly glide along,
Recovering breath, and pleased to win
The praises of mild Benjamin.

Good and Bad Children

ROBERT LOUIS STEVENSON

Children, you are very little
And your bones are very brittle;
If you would grow great and stately,
You must try to walk sedately.

You must still be bright and quiet,
And content with simple diet;
And remain, through all bewild'ring,
Innocent and honest children.

Happy hearts and happy faces,
Happy play in grassy places —
That was how, in ancient ages,
Children grew to kings and sages.

But the unkind and the unruly,
And the sort who eat unduly,
They must never hope for glory —
Theirs is quite a different story!

Cruel children, crying babies,
All grow up as geese and gabies,
Hated, as their age increases,
By their nephews and their nieces.

To-day

THOMAS CARLYLE

So here hath been dawning
Another blue day:
Think, wilt thou let it
Slip useless away?

Out of Eternity
This new day is born:
In to Eternity
At night will return.

Behold it aforetime
No eye ever did:
So soon it for ever
From all eyes is hid.

Here hath been dawning
Another blue day:
Think, wilt thou let it
Slip useless away?

The Sluggard

ISAAC WATTS

'Tis the voice of the sluggard; I hear him complain,
'You have waked me too soon: I must slumber again.'
　As the door on its hinges, so he on his bed,
　Turns his sides, and his shoulders, and his heavy head.

'A little more sleep, and a little more slumber' –
Thus he wastes half his days, and his hours without number;
　And when he gets up, he sits folding his hands,
　Or walks about saunt'ring, or trifling he stands.

I passed by his garden, and saw the wild brier,
The thorn and the thistle grow broader and higher.
　The clothes that hang on him are turning to rags;
　And his money still wastes till he starves or he begs.

I made him a visit, still hoping to find
He had took better care for improving his mind.
　He told me his dreams, talked of eating and drinking,
　But he scarce reads his Bible, and never loves thinking.

Said I then to my heart: 'Here's a lesson for me;
That man's but a picture of what I might be;
　But thanks to my friends for their care in my breeding,
　Who taught me betimes to love working and reading.'

The Shepherd Boy's Song

JOHN BUNYAN

He that is down needs fear no fall,
    He that is low, no pride;
He that is humble ever shall
    Have God to be his guide.

I am content with what I have,
    Little be it or much:
And, Lord, contentment still I crave,
    Because thou savest such.

Fullness to such a burden is
    That go on pilgrimage:
Here little, and hereafter bliss,
    Is best from age to age.

Lullaby for a Naughty Girl

E. V. RIEU

Oh peace, my Penelope: slaps are the fate
Of all little girls who are born to be great;
And the greatest of Queens have all been little girls
And dried up their tears on their kerchiefs or curls.

Oh sleep; and your heart that has sobbed for so long
Will mend and grow merry and wake you to song;
For the world is a lovelier place than it seems,
And a smack cannot follow you into your dreams.

The dark Cleopatra was slapped on the head,
And she wept as she lay in her great golden bed;
But the dark Cleopatra woke up with a smile
As she thought of the little boats out on the Nile.

And Helen of Troy had many a smack:
She moaned and she murmured the Greek for 'Alack!'
But the sun rose in Argos, and wonderful joy
Came with the morning to Helen of Troy.

They sent Guinevere without supper to sleep
In her grey little room at the top of the Keep;
And the stars over Camelot waited and wept
Till the peeping moon told them that Guinevere slept.

There was grief in Castile and dismay in Madrid
When they slapped Isabella for something she did;
But she slept – and could laugh in the morning again
At the Dons of Castile, the Hidalgos of Spain.

And oh, how Elizabeth cried in her cot
When she wanted her doll and her Nanny said not!
But the sparrows awoke and the summer sun rose,
And there was the doll on the bed by her toes!

So sleep, my Penelope: slaps are the fate
Of all little girls who are born to be great;
But the world is a lovelier place than it seems,
And a smack cannot follow you into your dreams.

Mr Nobody

ANONYMOUS

I know a funny little man,
  As quiet as a mouse.
He does the mischief that is done
  In everybody's house.
Though no one ever sees his face,
  Yet one and all agree
That every plate we break, was cracked
  By Mr Nobody.

'Tis he who always tears our books,
  Who leaves the door ajar.
He picks the buttons from our shirts,
  And scatters pins afar.
That squeaking door will always squeak –
  For prithee, don't you see?
We leave the oiling to be done
  By Mr Nobody.

He puts damp wood upon the fire,
  That kettles will not boil:
His are the feet that bring in mud
  And all the carpets soil.
The papers that so oft are lost –
  Who had them last but he?
There's no one tosses them about
  But Mr Nobody.

The fingermarks upon the door
  By none of us were made.
We never leave the blinds unclosed
  To let the curtains fade.

The ink we never spill! The boots
    That lying round you see,
Are not our boots – they all belong
    To Mr Nobody.

Matilda

who told lies, and was burned to death

HILAIRE BELLOC

Matilda told such Dreadful Lies,
It made one Gasp and Stretch one's Eyes;
Her Aunt, who from her Earliest Youth,
Had kept a Strict Regard for Truth,
Attempted to Believe Matilda:
The effort very nearly killed her,
And would have done so, had not She
Discovered this Infirmity.
For once, towards the Close of Day,
Matilda, growing tired of play,
And finding she was left alone,
Went tiptoe to the Telephone
And summoned the Immediate Aid
Of London's Noble Fire-Brigade.
Within an hour the Gallant Band
Were pouring in on every hand,
From Putney, Hackney Downs and Bow.
With Courage high and Hearts a-glow,
They galloped, roaring through the Town,
'Matilda's House is Burning Down!'
Inspired by British Cheers and Loud
Proceeding from the Frenzied Crowd,
They ran their ladders through a score
Of windows on the Ball Room Floor;
And took Peculiar Pains to Souse
The Pictures up and down the House,
Until Matilda's Aunt succeeded
In showing them they were not needed;
And even then she had to pay
To get the Men to go away!

It happened that a few Weeks later
Her Aunt was off to the Theatre
To see that Interesting Play
The Second Mrs Tanqueray.
She had refused to take her Niece
To hear that Entertaining Piece:
A Deprivation Just and Wise
To Punish her for Telling Lies.
That Night a Fire DID break out –
You should have heard Matilda Shout!
You should have heard her Scream and Bawl,
And throw the window up and call
To People passing in the Street –
(The rapidly increasing Heat
Encouraging her to obtain
Their confidence) – but all in vain!
For every time She shouted 'Fire!'
They only answered 'Little Liar!'
And therefore when her Aunt returned,
Matilda, and the House, were Burned.

Down in Yonder Meadow

ANONYMOUS

Down in yonder meadow where the green grass grows,
Pretty Pollie Pillicote bleaches her clothes.
She sang, she sang, she sang, oh, so sweet,
She sang, *Oh, come over!* across the street.

He kissed her, he kissed her, he bought her a gown,
A gown of rich cramasie out of the town.
He bought her a gown and a guinea gold ring,
A guinea, a guinea, a guinea gold ring.

Up street, and down, shine the windows made of glass,
Oh, isn't Pollie Pillicote a braw young lass?
Cherries in her cheeks, and ringlets in her hair,
Hear her singing *Handy Dandy* up and down the stair.

5 · HOLIDAY MOOD

—

Travelling

ANONYMOUS

One leg in front of the other,
One leg in front of the other,
  As the little dog travelled
  From London to Dover.
And when he came to a stile –
  Jump! he went over.

One More River

ANONYMOUS

The animals came in two by two,
    Vive la compagnie.
The centipede with the kangaroo.
    Vive la compagnie!
      One more river, and that's the river of Jordan,
    One more river, there's one more river to cross.

The animals came in three by three,
    Vive la compagnie.
The elephant on the back of the flea.
    Vive la compagnie!
    One more river, etc.

The animals came in four by four,
    Vive la compagnie.
The camel, he got stuck in the door.
    Vive la compagnie!
     One more river, etc.

The animals came in five by five,
    Vive la compagnie.
Some were dead and some were alive.
    Vive la compagnie!
     One more river, etc.

The animals came in six by six,
    Vive la compagnie.
The monkey, he was up to his tricks.
    Vive la compagnie!
     One more river, etc.

The animals came in seven by seven,
  Vive la compagnie.
Some went to Hell, and some went to Heaven.
  Vive la compagnie!
    One more river, etc.

The animals came in eight by eight,
  Vive la compagnie.
The worm was early, the bird was late.
  Vive la compagnie!
    One more river, etc.

The animals came in nine by nine,
  Vive la compagnie.
Some had water and some had wine.
  Vive la compagnie!
    One more river, etc.

The animals came in ten by ten,
  Vive la compagnie.
If you want any more you must sing it again.
  Vive la compagnie!
    One more river, and that's the river of Jordan,
    One more river, there's one more river to cross.

Lavender's Blue

ANONYMOUS

Lavender's blue, dilly dilly: lavender's green;
When I am King, dilly dilly, you shall be Queen.
Who told you that, dilly dilly, who told you so?
'Twas my own heart, dilly dilly, that told me so

Call up your men, dilly dilly, set them to work;
Some to the plough, dilly dilly, some to the cart;
Some to make hay, dilly dilly, some to thresh corn,
While you and I, dilly dilly, keep ourselves warm.

If I should die, dilly dilly, as well may hap,
Bury me deep, dilly dilly, under the tap;
Under the tap, dilly dilly, I'll tell you why,
That I may drink, dilly dilly, when I am dry.

Girls and Boys Come out to Play

ANONYMOUS

Girls and boys come out to play,
The moon doth shine as bright as day!

Leave your supper and leave your sleep,
Come with your playfellows into the street.

Come with a whistle, come with a call,
Come with a good will or come not at all.

Up the ladder and down the wall,
A halfpenny roll will serve us all.

You find milk and I'll find flour,
And we'll have a pudding in half an hour.

The Three Jovial Huntsmen

ANONYMOUS

There were three jovial Welshmen,
  As I have heard men say,
And they would go a-hunting, boys,
  Upon St David's Day.
And all the day they hunted,
  But nothing could they find,
Except a ship a-sailing
  A-sailing with the wind.
    And a-hunting they did go.

One said it surely was a ship,
  The second he said, Nay;
The third declared it was a house
  With the chimney blown away.
Then all the night they hunted,
  And nothing could they find,
Except the moon a-gliding,
  A-gliding with the wind.
    And a-hunting they did go.

One said it surely was the moon,
  The second he said, Nay;
The third declared it was a cheese,
  The half o' it cut away.
Then all next day they hunted,
  And nothing could they find,
Except a hedgehog in a bush,
  And that they left behind.
    And a-hunting they did go.

One said it was a hedgehog,
  The second he said, Nay;
The third, it was a pincushion,
  The pins stuck in wrong way.
Then all next night they hunted,
  And nothing could they find,
Except a hare in a turnip field,
  And that they left behind.
    And a-hunting they did go.

One said it surely was a hare,
  The second he said, Nay;
The third he said it was a calf,
  And the cow had run away.
Then all next day they hunted,
  And nothing could they find,
But one owl in a holly-tree,
  And that they left behind.
    And a-hunting they did go.

One said it surely was an owl,
  The second he said, Nay;
The third said 'twas an aged man
  Whose beard was growing grey.
Then all three jovial Welshmen
  Came riding home at last,
'For three days we have nothing killed,
  And never broke our fast!'
    And a-hunting they did go.

To my Sister

WILLIAM WORDSWORTH

It is the first mild day of March:
Each minute sweeter than before,
The redbreast sings from the tall larch
That stands beside our door.

There is a blessing in the air,
Which seems a sense of joy to yield
To the bare trees, and mountains bare,
And grass in the green field.

My sister! ('tis a wish of mine)
Now that our morning meal is done,
Make haste, your morning task resign;
Come forth and feel the sun.

Edward will come with you – and pray,
Put on with speed your woodland dress;
And bring no book: for this one day
We'll give to idleness.

Weathers

THOMAS HARDY

This is the weather the cuckoo likes,
    And so do I;
When showers betumble the chestnut spikes,
    And nestlings fly;
And the little brown nightingale bills his best,
And they sit outside at 'The Travellers' Rest',
And maids come forth sprig-muslin drest,
And citizens dream of the south and west,
    And so do I.

This is the weather the shepherd shuns,
    And so do I;
When beeches drip in browns and duns,
    And thresh, and ply;
And hill-hid tides throb, throe on throe,
And meadow rivulets overflow,
And drops on gate-bars hang in a row,
And rooks in families homeward go,
    And so do I.

Fisherman's Lore

ANONYMOUS

When the wind is in the East
'Tis neither good for man nor beast.

When the wind is in the North
The skilful fisher goes not forth.

When the wind is in the South
It blows the bait in the fish's mouth.

When the wind is in the West,
Then it is at its very best.

The Owl and the Pussy-Cat

EDWARD LEAR

The Owl and the Pussy-Cat went to sea
    In a beautiful pea-green boat,
They took some honey, and plenty of money,
    Wrapped up in a five-pound note.
The Owl looked up to the stars above,
    And sang to a small guitar,
'O lovely Pussy! O Pussy, my love,
    What a beautiful Pussy you are,
        You are,
        You are,
    What a beautiful Pussy you are!'

Puss said to the Owl, 'You elegant fowl!
    How charmingly sweet you sing!
O let us be married! too long we have tarried:
    But what shall we do for a ring?'
They sailed away for a year and a day,
    To the land where the Bong-tree grows,
And there in a wood a Piggy-wig stood,
    With a ring at the end of his nose,
        His nose,
        His nose,
    With a ring at the end of his nose.

'Dear Pig, are you willing to sell for one shilling,
Your ring?' Said the Piggy, 'I will.'
So they took it away, and were married next day
    By the Turkey who lived on the hill.
They dined on mince, and slices of quince,
    Which they ate with a runcible spoon;
And hand in hand, on the edge of the sand,

They danced by the light of the moon,
   The moon,
   The moon,
They danced by the light of the moon.

Two Limericks

EDWARD LEAR

There was an Old Man with a beard,
Who said, 'It is just as I feared!
   Two Owls and a Hen,
   Four Larks and a Wren
Have all built their nests in my beard!'

*   *   *

There was an Old Lady whose folly
Induced her to sit in a holly:
   Whereupon by a thorn
   Her dress being torn,
She quickly became melancholy.

The Strange Wild Song

FROM *Sylvie and Bruno*

LEWIS CARROLL

He thought he saw a Buffalo,
　　Upon the chimney-piece:
He looked again, and found it was
　　His Sister's Husband's Niece.
'Unless you leave this house,' he said,
　　'I'll send for the Police!'

He thought he saw a Rattlesnake,
　　That questioned him in Greek;
He looked again, and found it was
　　The Middle of Next Week.
'The one thing I regret,' he said,
　　'Is that it cannot speak!'

He thought he saw a Banker's Clerk
　　Descending from a bus;
He looked again, and found it was
　　A Hippopotamus.
'If this should stay to dine,' he said,
　　'There won't be much for us!'

He thought he saw a Kangaroo
　　That worked a coffee mill;
He looked again, and found it was
　　A Vegetable Pill.
'Were I to swallow this,' he said,
　　'I should be very ill!'

He thought he saw a Coach-and-four
   That stood beside his bed;
He looked again, and found it was
   A Bear without a Head;
'Poor thing,' he said, 'poor silly thing!
   It's waiting to be fed!'

He thought he saw an Albatross
   That fluttered round the Lamp;
He looked again, and found it was
   A Penny-Postage-Stamp.
'You'd best be getting home,' he said,
   'The nights are very damp!'

Striking

CHARLES STUART CALVERLEY

It was a railway passenger,
　　And he lept out jauntilie,
'Now up and bear, thou stout porter,
　　My two chattèls to me.

'Bring hither, bring hither my bag so red,
　　And portmanteau so brown;
They lie in the van, for a trusty man,
　　He labelled them London town.

'And fetch me eke a cabman bold,
　　That I may be his fare, his fare;
And he shall have a good shilling,
If by two of the clock he do me bring,
　　To the terminus, Euston Square.'

'Now, so to the saints alway,
　　Good gentleman, give luck,
As never a cab may I find this day,
　　For the cabman wights have struck.'

'Now rede me aright, thou stout porter,
　　What were it best I should do;
For woe is me an I reach not there,
　　Or ever the clock strike two.'

'I have a son, a lytel son;
　　Fleet is his foot as the wild roebuck's;
Give him a shilling and eke a brown,
And he shall carry thy fardels down
To Euston, or half over London town,
　　On one of the station trucks.'

Then forth in a hurry they twain did fare,
   The gent and the porter's son,
Who fled like an arrow nor turned a hair,
   Thro' all the mire and the muck.

'A ticket, a ticket, Sir Clerk, I pray;
   For by two of the clock must I needs away.'
'O that may hardly be,' quoth the Clerk,
   'For already, indeed, the clocks have struck!'

Yarrow Unvisited

WILLIAM WORDSWORTH

From Stirling Castle we had seen
The mazy Forth unravelled;
Had trod the banks of Clyde and Tay,
And with the Tweed had travelled;
And when we came to Clovenford,
Then said my *winsome Marrow*,
'Whate'er betide, we'll turn aside,
And see the Braes of Yarrow.'

'Let Yarrow folk, *frae* Selkirk Town,
Who have been buying, selling,
Go back to Yarrow, 'tis their own;
Each maiden to her dwelling!
On Yarrow's banks let herons feed,
Hares couch, and rabbits burrow,
But we will downward with the Tweed,
Nor turn aside to Yarrow.

'There's Gala Water, Leader Haughs,
Both lying right before us;
And Dryburgh, where with chiming Tweed
The lintwhites sing in chorus.
There's pleasant Teviotdale, a land
Made blithe with plough and harrow:
Why throw away a needful day,
To go in search of Yarrow?

'What's Yarrow but a river bare,
That glides the dark hills under?
There are a thousand such elsewhere
As worthy of your wonder.'

– Strange words they seemed, of slight and scorn;
My True-love sighed for sorrow;
And looked me in the face, to think
I thus could speak of Yarrow!

'Oh! green,' said I, 'are Yarrow's holms,
And sweet is Yarrow flowing!
Fair hangs the apple frae the rock,
But we will leave it growing!
O'er hilly path, and open Strath,
We'll wander Scotland thorough;
But, though so near, we will not turn
Into the dale of Yarrow.

'Let beeves and home-bred kine partake
The sweets of Burn-mill meadow;
The swan on still St Mary's Lake
Float double, swan and shadow!
We will not see them, will not go,
To-day, nor yet to-morrow;
Enough if in our hearts we know
There's such a place as Yarrow.'

The Vagabond

ROBERT LOUIS STEVENSON

Give to me the life I love,
  Let the lave go by me,
Give the jolly heaven above
  And the byway nigh me.
Bed in the bush with stars to see,
  Bread I dip in the river —
There's the life for a man like me,
  There's the life for ever.

Let the blow fall soon or late,
  Let what will be o'er me;
Give the face of earth around
  And the road before me.
Wealth I seek not, hope nor love,
  Nor a friend to know me;
All I seek, the heaven above
  And the road below me.

Or let autumn fall on me
  Where afield I linger,
Silencing the bird on tree,
  Biting the blue finger.
White as meal the frosty field —
  Warm the fireside haven —
Not to autumn will I yield,
  Not to winter even!

Let the blow fall soon or late,
  Let what will be o'er me;
Give the face of earth around,
  And the road before me.

Wealth I ask not, hope nor love,
  Nor a friend to know me;
All I ask, the heaven above,
  And the road below me.

Home-Thoughts, from Abroad

ROBERT BROWNING

O to be in England
Now that April's there,
And whoever wakes in England
Sees, some morning, unaware,
That the lowest boughs and the brushwood sheaf
Round the elm-tree bole are in tiny leaf,
While the chaffinch sings on the orchard bough
In England – now!

And after April, when May follows,
And the whitethroat builds, and all the swallows!
Hark, where my blossom'd pear-tree in the hedge
Leans to the field and scatters on the clover
Blossoms and dewdrops – at the bent spray's edge –
That's the wise thrush; he sings each song twice over
Lest you should think he never could recapture
The first fine careless rapture!
And though the fields look rough with hoary dew,
All will be gay when noontide wakes anew
The buttercups, the little children's dower
– Far brighter than this gaudy melon-flower!

The Bells of London

ANONYMOUS

Gay go up and gay go down
To ring the bells of London Town!

Bull's eyes and targets,
Say the bells of St Marg'rets.

Brickbats and tiles,
Say the bells of St Giles.

Halfpence and farthings,
Say the bells of St Martins.

Oranges and lemons,
Say the bells of St Clement's.

Pokers and tongs,
Say the bells of St John's.

Tin kettles and saucepans,
Say the bells of St Anne's.

Old father Baldpate,
Say the slow bells of Aldgate.

You owe me ten shillings,
Say the bells of St Helen's.

When will you pay me?
Say the bells of Old Bailey.

When I grow rich,
Say the bells of Shoreditch.

When will that be?
Say the bells of Stepney.

I'm sure I don't know,
Says the great bell at Bow.

The End of the Road

FROM *The Path to Rome*

HILAIRE BELLOC

In these boots and with this staff
Two hundred leaguers and a half
Walked I, went I, paced I, tripped I,
Marched I, held I, skelped I, slipped I,
Pushed I, panted, swung and dashed I;
Picked I, forded, swam and splashed I,
Strolled I, climbed I, crawled and scrambled,
Dropped and dipped I, ranged and rambled;
Plodded I, hobbled I, trudged and tramped I,
And in lonely spinnies camped I,
Lingered, loitered, limped and crept I,
Clambered, halted, stepped and leapt I,
Slowly sauntered, roundly strode I,
And . . .
Let me not conceal it . . . rode I.

(For who but critics could complain
Of 'riding' in a railway train?)

Across the valleys and the high land,
With all the world on either hand,
Drinking when I had a mind to,
Singing when I felt inclined to;
Nor ever turned my face to home
Till I had slaked my heart at Rome.

Adlestrop

EDWARD THOMAS

Yes. I remember Adlestrop –
The name, because one afternoon
Of heat, the express-train drew up there
Unwontedly. It was late June.

The steam hissed. Someone cleared his throat.
No one left and no one came
On the bare platform. What I saw
Was Aldestrop – only the name

And willows, willow-herb, and grass,
And meadowsweet, and haycocks dry,
No whit less still and lonely fair
Than the high cloudlets in the sky.

And for that minute a blackbird sang
Close by, and round him, mistier,
Farther and farther, all the birds
Of Oxfordshire and Gloucestershire.

Sing me a Song

ROBERT LOUIS STEVENSON

Sing me a song of a lad that is gone,
  Say, could that lad be I?
Merry of soul he sailed on a day
  Over the sea to Skye.

Mull was astern, Rum on the port,
  Eigg on the starboard bow;
Glory of youth glowed in his soul:
  Where is that glory now?

Sing me a song of a lad that is gone,
  Say, could that lad be I?
Merry of soul he sailed on a day
  Over the sea to Skye.

Give me again all that was there,
  Give me the sun that shone!
Give me the eyes, give me the soul,
  Give me the lad that's gone!

Sing me a song of a lad that is gone,
  Say, could that lad be I?
Merry of soul he sailed on a day
  Over the sea to Skye.

Billow and breeze, islands and seas,
  Mountains of rain and sun,
All that was good, all that was fair,
  All that was me is gone.

6 · MAGIC AND ROMANCE

—

I had a Little Nut Tree

ANONYMOUS

I had a little nut-tree,
  Nothing would it bear
But a silver nutmeg
  And a golden pear.

The King of Spain's daughter
  Came to visit me,
All for the sake
  Of my little nut-tree.

I skipped over ocean,
  I danced over sea;
And all the birds in the air
  Couldn't catch me!

How Many Miles to Babylon?

ANONYMOUS

How many miles to Babylon?
Threescore and ten, Sir.

Can I get there by candlelight?
Oh yes, and back again, Sir.

If your heels are nimble and light,
You may get there by candlelight.

He Loves me – He Loves me Not

ANONYMOUS

One I love, two I love,
Three I love I say;
Four I love with all my heart,
Five I cast away.
   Six he loves, seven she loves,
    Eight they love together;
   Nine he comes, ten he tarries,
    Eleven he woos, and twelve he marries.

Lament

ANONYMOUS

Wae's me, wae's me!
The acorn's not yet
Fallen from the tree
That's to grow the wood,
That's to make the cradle,
That's to rock the bairn,
That'll grow to the man
Who's to lay me!

Some One

WALTER DE LA MARE

Some one came knocking
　At my wee, small door;
Some one came knocking,
　I'm sure – sure – sure;

I listened, I opened,
　I looked to left and right,
But nought there was a-stirring
　In the still dark night;

Only the busy beetle
　Tap-tapping in the wall,
Only from the forest
　The screech-owl's call,

Only the cricket whistling
　While the dewdrops fall,
So I know not who came knocking,
　At all, at all, at all.

London Bridge is Broken Down

ANONYMOUS

London Bridge is broken down,
Dance o'er my Lady Lee;
London Bridge is broken down,
With a gay lady.

How shall we build it up again?
Dance o'er my Lady Lee;
How shall we build it up again?
With a gay lady.

Silver and gold will be stole away,
Dance o'er my Lady Lee;
Silver and gold will be stole away,
With a gay lady.

Build it up with iron and steel,
Dance o'er my Lady Lee;
Build it up with iron and steel,
With a gay lady.

Iron and steel will bend and bow,
Dance o'er my Lady Lee;
Iron and steel will bend and bow,
With a gay lady.

Build it up with wood and clay,
Dance o'er my Lady Lee;
Build it up with wood and clay,
With a gay lady.

Wood and clay will wash away,
Dance o'er my Lady Lee;
Wood and clay will wash away,
With a gay lady.

Build it up with stone so strong,
Dance o'er my Lady Lee;
Build it up with stone so strong,
With a gay lady.

The Fairies

WILLIAM ALLINGHAM

Up the airy mountain,
    Down the rushy glen,
We daren't go a-hunting
    For fear of little men;
Wee folk, good folk,
    Trooping all together;
Green jacket, red cap,
    And white owl's feather!

Down along the rocky shore
    Some make their home;
They live on crispy pancakes
    Of yellow tide-foam;
Some in the reeds
    Of the black mountain lake,
With frogs for their watch-dogs,
    All night awake.

High on the hill-top
    The old King sits;
He is now so old and grey
    He's nigh lost his wits.
With a bridge of white mist
    Columbkill he crosses,
On his stately journeys
    From Slieveleague to Rosses;
Or going up with music
    On cold starry nights,
To sup with the Queen
    Of the gay Northern Lights.

They stole little Bridget
  For seven years long;
When she came down again,
  Her friends were all gone.
They took her lightly back,
  Between the night and morrow,
They thought that she was fast asleep,
  But she was dead with sorrow.
They have kept her ever since
  Deep within the lake,
On a bed of flag-leaves,
Watching till she wake.

By the craggy hill-side,
  Through the mosses bare,
They have planted thorn-trees
  For pleasure here and there.
Is any man so daring
  As dig them up in spite,
He shall find the thornies set
  In his bed at night.

Up the airy mountain,
  Down the rushy glen,
We daren't go a-hunting
  For fear of little men;
Wee folk, good folk,
  Trooping all together;
Green jacket, red cap,
  And white owl's feather!

Proud Maisie

SIR WALTER SCOTT

Proud Maisie is in the wood,
   Walking so early;
Sweet Robin sits on the bush,
   Singing so rarely.

'Tell me, thou bonny bird,
   When shall I marry me?'
'When six braw gentlemen
   Kirkward shall carry ye.'

'Who makes the bridal bed,
   Birdie, say truly?'
'The grey-headed sexton,
   That delves the grave duly.

'The glow-worm o'er grave and stone
   Shall light thee steady;
The owl from the steeple sing,
   "Welcome, proud lady!"'

Sevens

ELEANOR FARJEON

Seven Sisters in patchwork cloaks
Sat in the shadow of Seven Oaks,
   Stringing acorns on silken strings,
   Awaiting the coming of Seven Kings.

Seven years they endured their trials
And then they consulted their Seven Dials.
   'O it's time, it's time, it's time,' they said,
   'It's very high time that we were wed!'

Locksley Hall

ALFRED LORD TENNYSON

Comrades, leave me here a little, while as yet 'tis early morn:
Leave me here, and when you want me, sound upon the bugle-horn.

'Tis the place, and all around it, as of old, the curlews call,
Dreary gleams about the moorland, flying over Locksley Hall;

Locksley Hall, that in the distance overlooks the sandy tracts,
And the hollow ocean-ridges roaring into cataracts.

Many a night from yonder ivied casement, ere I went to rest,
Did I look on great Orion sloping slowly to the West.

Many a night I saw the Pleiads, rising thro' the mellow shade,
Glitter like a swarm of fire-flies tangled in a silver braid.

Here about the beach I wandered, nourishing a youth sublime
With the fairy tales of science, and the long result of Time;

When the centuries behind me like a fruitful land reposed;
When I clung to all the present for the promise that it closed;

When I dipped into the future far as human eye could see;
Saw the Vision of the world, and all the wonder that would be.

Kubla Khan

SAMUEL TAYLOR COLERIDGE

In Xanadu did Kubla Khan
  A stately pleasure-dome decree;
Where Alph, the sacred river, ran
Through caverns measureless to man
  Down to a sunless sea.

So twice five miles of fertile ground
With walls and towers were girdled round;
And here were gardens bright with sinuous rills
Where blossomed many an incense-bearing tree;
And here were forests ancient as the hills,
Enfolding sunny spots of greenery.

But O, that deep romantic chasm which slanted
Down the green hill athwart a cedarn cover!
A savage place! as holy and enchanted
As e'er beneath a waning moon was haunted
By woman wailing for her demon-lover!
And from this chasm, with ceaseless turmoil seething,
As if this earth in fast thick pants were breathing,
A mighty fountain momently was forced;
Amid whose swift half-intermitted burst
Huge fragments vaulted like rebounding hail,
Or chaffy grain beneath the thresher's flail:
And 'mid these dancing rocks at once and ever:
It flung up momently the sacred river.
Five miles meandering with a mazy motion
Through wood and dale the sacred river ran,
Then reached the caverns measureless to man,
And sank in tumult to a lifeless ocean:

And 'mid this tumult Kubla heard from far
Ancestral voices prophesying war!

   The shadow of the dome of pleasure
   Floated midway on the waves;
   Where was heard the mingled measure
   From the fountain and the caves.
It was a miracle of rare device,
A sunny pleasure-dome with caves of ice!
A damsel with a dulcimer
In a vision once I saw:
It was an Abyssinian maid,
And on her dulcimer she played,
Singing of Mount Abora.
Could I revive within me
Her sympathy and song,
To such a deep delight 'twould win me,
That with music loud and long,
I would build that dome in air,
That sunny dome! those caves of ice!
And all who heard should see them there,
And all should cry, Beware! Beware!
His flashing eyes, his floating hair!
Weave a circle round him thrice,
And close your eyes with holy dread,
For he on honey-dew hath fed,
And drunk the milk of Paradise.

The Lady of Shalott

ALFRED LORD TENNYSON

On either side the river lie
Long fields of barley and of rye,
That clothe the wold and meet the sky;
And thro' the field the road runs by
    To many-tower'd Camelot;
And up and down the people go,
Gazing where the lilies blow
Round an island there below,
    The island of Shalott.

Willows whiten, aspens quiver,
Little breezes dusk and shiver
Thro' the wave that runs for ever
By the island in the river
    Flowing down to Camelot.
Four grey walls, and four grey towers,
Overlook a space of flowers,
And the silent isle embowers
    The Lady of Shalott.

By the margin, willow-veil'd,
Slide the heavy barges trail'd
By slow horses; and unhail'd
The shallop flitteth, silken-sail'd
    Skimming down to Camelot:
But who hath seen her wave her hand?
Or at the casement seen her stand?
Or is she known in all the land,
    The Lady of Shalott?

Only reapers, reaping early
In among the bearded barley,
Hear a song that echoes cheerly
From the river winding clearly,
    Down to tower'd Camelot:
And by the moon the reaper weary,
Piling sheaves in uplands airy,
Listening, whispers, 'Tis the fairy
    Lady of Shalott.'

The High Tide on the Coast of Lincolnshire

JEAN INGELOW

I shall never hear her more
By the reedy Lindis shore,
'Cusha! Cusha! Cusha!' calling,
Ere the early dews be falling:
I shall never hear her song,
'Cusha! Cusha!' all along
Where the sunny Lindis floweth,
    Goeth, floweth;
From the meads where melick groweth,
When the water winding down,
Onward floweth to the town.

I shall never see her more
Where the reeds and rushes quiver,
    Shiver, quiver;
Stand beside the sobbing river,
Sobbing, throbbing, in its falling
To the sandy lonesome shore;
I shall never hear her calling,
  'Leave your meadow grasses mellow,
    Mellow, mellow;
  Quit your cowslips, cowslips yellow;
  Come up Whitefoot, come up Lightfoot;
  Quit your pipes of parsley hollow,
    Hollow, hollow;
  Come up Lightfoot, rise and follow;
    Lightfoot, Whitefoot,
  From your clovers lift the head;
  Come up Jetty, follow, follow,
  Jetty, to the milking shed.'

New Year's Chimes

FRANCIS THOMPSON

What is the song the stars sing?
  (*And a million songs are as song of one*)
This is the song the stars sing:
  (*Sweeter song's none*)

One to set, and many to sing,
  (*And a million songs are as song of one*)
One to stand and many to cling,
The many things, and the one Thing,
  The one that runs not, the many that run.

The ever new weaveth the ever old,
  (*And a million songs are as song of one*)
Ever telling the never told,
The silver saith, and the said is gold,
  And done ever, the never done.

To S. R. Crockett

ROBERT LOUIS STEVENSON

Blows the wind to-day, and the sun and the rain are flying,
  Blows the wind on the moors to-day and now,
Where about the graves of the martyrs the whaups are crying,
  My heart remembers how!

Grey recumbent tombs of the dead in desert places,
  Standing stones on the vacant wine-red moor,
Hills of sheep, and the howes of the silent vanished races,
  And winds, austere and pure.

Be it granted me to behold you again in dying,
  Hills of home! and to hear again the call;
Hear about the graves of the martyrs the peewees crying,
  And hear no more at all.

The Mad Maid's Song

ROBERT HERRICK

Good-morrow to the day so fair,
    Good morning, Sir, to you;
Good-morrow to mine own torn hair
    Bedabbled with the dew.

Good morning to this primrose too,
    Good-morrow to each maid;
That will with flowers the tomb bestrew
    Wherein my love is laid.

Ah! woe is me, woe, woe is me!
    Alack and well-a-day!
For pity, Sir, find out that bee
    Which bore my love away.

I'll seek him in your bonnet brave,
    I'll seek him in your eyes;
Nay, now I think they've made his grave
    I' th' bed of strawberries.

I'll seek him there; I know, ere this
    The cold, cold earth doth shake him;
But I will go, or send a kiss
    By you, Sir, to awake him.

Pray hurt him not; though he be dead
    He knows well who do love him,
And who with green turfs rear his head,
    And who do rudely move him.

He's soft and tender (pray take heed);
    With bands of cowslips bind him,
And bring him home, but 'tis decreed
    That I shall never find him.

The Song of the Mad Prince

WALTER DE LA MARE

Who said, 'Peacock Pie'?
  The old King to the sparrow:
Who said, 'Crops are ripe'?
  Rust to the harrow:
Who said, 'Where sleeps she now?
  Where rests she now her head,
Bathed in Eve's loveliness'? –
  That's what I said.

Who said, 'Ay, mum's the word';
  Sexton to willow:
Who said, 'Green dusk for dreams,
  Moss for a pillow'?
Who said, 'All Time's delight
  Hath she for narrow bed;
Life's troubled bubble broken'? –
  That's what I said.

A Lyke-Wake Dirge

ANONYMOUS

This ae night, this ae night,
Every night and all;
Fire and sleete and candle light,
And Christ receive thy saul.

When thou from hence away art past,
Every night and all;
To Whinny-muir thou comest at last;
And Christ receive thy saul.

If ever thou gavest hosen and shoon,
Every night and all;
Sit thee down and put them on;
And Christ receive thy saul.

If hosen and shoon thou ne'er gavest nane,
Every night and all;
The whinnes shall prick thee to the bare bane
And Christ receive thy saul.

From Whinny-muir when thou mayest pass,
Every night and all;
To Brigg o' Dread thou comest at last;
Then Christ receive thy saul.

From Brigg o' Dread when thou mayest pass,
Every night and all;
To purgatory fire thou comest at last;
And Christ receive thy saul.

If ever thou gavest meat or drink,
Every night and all;
The fire shall never make thee shrink;
And Christ receive thy saul.

If meat or drink thou never gavest nane,
  Every night and all;
The fire will burn thee to the bare bane;
  And Christ receive thy saul.

This ae night, this ae night,
  Every night and all;
Fire and sleete and candle light;
  And Christ receive thy saul.

Meet-on-the-Road

ANONYMOUS

'Now, pray, where are you going?' said Meet-on-the-Road.
'To school, sir, to school sir,' said Child-as-it-Stood.

'What have you in your basket, child?' said Meet-on-the-Road.
'My dinner, sir, my dinner, sir,' said Child-as-it-Stood.

'What have you for dinner child?' said Meet-on-the-Road.
'Some pudding, sir, some pudding, sir,' said Child-as-it-Stood.

'Oh, then I pray, give me a share,' said Meet-on-the-Road.
'I've little enough for myself, sir,' said Child-as-it-Stood.

'What have you got that cloak on for?' said Meet-on-the-Road.
'To keep the wind and cold from me,' said Child-as-it-Stood.

'I wish the wind would blow through you,' said Meet-on-the-Road.
'Oh, what a wish! What a wish!' said Child-as-it-Stood.

'Pray what are those bells ringing for?' said Meet-on-the-Road.
'To ring bad spirits home again,' said Child-as-it-Stood.

'Oh, then I must be going, child!' said Meet-on-the-Road.
'So fare you well, so fare you well,' said Child-as-it-Stood.

Alms in Autumn

ROSE FYLEMAN

Spindlewood, spindlewood, will you lend me pray,
A little flaming lantern to guide me on my way?
The fairies all have vanished from the meadow and the glen,
And I would fain go seeking till I find them once again.
Lend me now a lantern that I may bear a light,
To find the hidden pathway in the darkness of the night.

Ashtree, ashtree, throw me, if you please,
Throw me down a slender bunch of russet-gold keys,
I fear the gates of Fairyland may all be shut so fast
That nothing but your magic keys will ever take me past.
I'll tie them to my girdle and as I go along,
My heart will find a comfort in the tinkle of their song.

Hollybush, hollybush, help me in my task,
A pocketful of berries is all the alms I ask,
A pocketful of berries to thread on golden strands,
(I would not go a-visiting with nothing in my hands).
So fine will be the rosy chains, so gay, so glossy bright,
They'll set the realms of Fairyland all dancing with delight.

Jim Jay

WALTER DE LA MARE

Do diddle di do,
  Poor Jim Jay
Got stuck fast
  In Yesterday.
Squinting he was,
  On cross-legs bent,
Never heeding
  The wind was spent.
Round veered the weathercock,
  The sun drew in –
And stuck was Jim
  Like a rusty pin . . .
We pulled and we pulled
  From seven till twelve,
Jim, too frightened
  To help himself.
But all in vain.
  The clock struck one,
And there was Jim
  A little bit gone.
At half-past five
  You scarce could see
A glimpse of his flapping
  Handkerchee.
And when came noon,
  And we climbed sky-high,
Jim was a speck
  Slip-slipping by.

Come to-morrow,
  The neighbours say,
He'll be past crying for;
  Poor Jim Jay.

Romance

W. J. TURNER

When I was but thirteen or so
  I went into a golden land;
Chimborazo, Cotopaxi
  Took me by the hand.

My father died, my brother too,
  They passed like fleeting dreams.
I stood where Popocatapetl
  In the sunlight gleams.

I dimly heard the master's voice
  And boys far off at play.
Chimborazo, Cotopaxi
  Had stolen me away.

I walked in a great golden dream
  To and fro from school –
Shining Popocatapetl
  The dusty streets did rule.

I walked home with a gold dark boy,
  And never a word I'd say,
Chimborazo, Cotopaxi
  Had taken my speech away:

I gazed entranced upon his face
  Fairer than any flower –
O shining Popocatapetl,
  It was thy magic hour:

The houses, people, traffic seemed
   Thin fading dreams by day,
Chimborazo, Cotopaxi
   They had stolen my soul away.

The Chimney Sweeper

WILLIAM BLAKE

When my mother died I was very young,
And my father sold me while yet my tongue
   Could scarcely cry, ' 'weep, 'weep! 'weep 'weep!'
   So your chimneys I sweep, and in soot I sleep.

There's little Tom Dacre, who cried when his head,
That curled like a lamb's back, was shaved: so I said,
   'Hush, Tom! never mind it, for when your head's bare
   You know that the soot cannot spoil your white hair.'

And so he was quiet, and that very night,
As Tom was a-sleeping, he had such a sight!
   That thousands of sweepers, Dick, Joe, Ned, and Jack,
   Were all of them lock'd up in coffins of black.

And by came an Angel who had a bright key,
And he opened the coffins and set them all free;
   Then down a green plain leaping, laughing they run,
   And wash in a river, and shine in the Sun.

Then naked and white, all their bags left behind,
They rise upon clouds and sport in the wind;
   And the Angel told Tom, if he'd be a good boy,
   He'd have God for his father, and never want joy.

And so Tom awoke; and we rose in the dark,
And got with our bags and our brushes to work.
   Though the morning was cold, Tom was happy and warm;
   So, if all do their duty, they need not fear harm.

Chamber Music

JAMES JOYCE

Lean out of the window,
  Golden hair,
I hear you singing
  A merry air.

My book is closed;
  I read no more,
Watching the fire dance
  On the floor.

I have left my books:
  I have left my room:
For I heard you singing
  Through the gloom.

Singing and singing
  A merry air.
Lean out of the window,
  Golden hair.

Why so Pale and Wan?

SIR JOHN SUCKLING

Why so pale and wan, fond lover?
  Prithee, why so pale?
Will, when looking well can't move her,
  Looking ill prevail?
  Prithee, why so pale?

Why so dull and mute, young sinner?
  Prithee, why so mute?
Will, when speaking well can't win her,
  Saying nothing do't?
  Prithee, why so mute?

Quit, quit for shame! This will not move;
  This cannot take her.
If of herself she will not love,
  Nothing can make her:
  The devil take her!

Epitaph Upon a Child that Died

ROBERT HERRICK

Here she lies, a pretty bud,
Lately made of flesh and blood:
Who as soon fell fast asleep,
As her little eyes did peep.
Give her strewings, but not stir
The earth, that lightly covers her.

Lines on a Clock in Chester Cathedral

HENRY TWELLS

When as a child, I laughed and wept,
    Time crept.
When as a youth, I dreamt and talked,
    Time walked.
When I became a full-grown man,
    Time ran.
When older still I daily grew,
    Time flew.
Soon I shall find on travelling on –
    Time gone.
O Christ, wilt Thou have saved me then?
    Amen.

7 · NIGHT

—

Day and Night

LADY LINDSAY

Said Day to Night,
'I bring God's light.
  What gift have you?'
  Night said, 'The dew.'

'I give bright hours,'
Quoth Day, 'and flowers.'
  Said Night, 'More blest,
  I bring sweet rest.'

The Stars at Night

JANE AND ANN TAYLOR

Twinkle, twinkle, little star,
How I wonder what you are!
Up above the world so high,
Like a diamond in the sky.

In the dark blue sky you keep
And often through my curtain peep,
For you never shut your eye
Till the sun is in the sky.

As your bright and tiny spark
Lights the traveller in the dark,
Though I know not what you are,
Twinkle, twinkle, little star.

A Night in June

WILLIAM WORDSWORTH

The sun has long been set,
  The stars are out by twos and threes,
The little birds are piping yet
  Among the bushes and the trees;
There's a cuckoo, and one or two thrushes,
And a far-off wind that rushes,
And a sound of water that gushes,
  And the cuckoo's sovereign cry
  Fills all the hollow of the sky.
Who would go 'parading'
In London, 'and masquerading',
  On such a night of June
  With that beautiful soft half-moon,
And all these innocent blisses?
On such a night as this is!

Windy Nights

ROBERT LOUIS STEVENSON

Whenever the moon and stars are set,
  Whenever the wind is high,
All night long in the dark and wet,
  A man goes riding by.
Late in the night when the fires are out,
Why does he gallop and gallop about?

Whenever the trees are crying aloud,
  And ships are tossed at sea,
By, on the highway, low and loud,
  By at the gallop goes he.
By at the gallop he goes, and then
By he comes back at the gallop again.

A Sea Burden

C. FOX SMITH

A ship swinging,
As the tide swings, up and down,
And men's voices singing,
    East away O! West away!
    And a very long way from London Town.

A lantern glowing
And the stars looking down,
And the sea smells blowing.
    East away O! West away!
    And a very long way from London Town.

Lights in wild weather
From a tavern window, old and brown,
And men singing together,
    East away O! West away!
    And a very long way from London Town.

Night

WILLIAM BLAKE

The sun descending in the west,
The evening star does shine;
The birds are silent in their nest,
And I must seek for mine.
   The moon, like a flower,
   In heaven's high bower,
   With silent delight
   Sits and smiles on the night.

Farewell, green fields and happy groves,
Where flocks have took delight;
Where lambs have nibbled, silent moves
The feet of angels bright;
   Unseen they pour blessing,
   And joy without ceasing,
   On each bud and blossom,
   And each sleeping bosom.

They look in every thoughtless nest,
Where birds are covered warm;
They visit caves of every beast,
To keep them all from harm.
   If they see any weeping,
   That should have been sleeping,
   They pour sleep on their head,
   And sit down by their bed.

When wolves and tigers howl for prey,
They pitying stand and weep;
Seeking to drive their thirst away,
And keep them from the sheep.

But if they rush dreadful,
The angels, most heedful,
Receive each mild spirit,
New worlds to inherit.

And there the lion's ruddy eyes
Shall flow with tears of gold,
And pitying the tender cries,
And walking round the fold,
　　Saying, 'Wrath, by his meekness,
　　And, by his health, sickness
　　Is driven away
　　From our immortal day.

'And now beside thee, bleating lamb,
I can lie down and sleep;
Or think on him who bore thy name,
Graze after thee and weep.
　　For, washed in life's river,
　　My bright mane for ever
　　Shall shine like the gold,
　　As I guard o'er the fold.'

Ode to a Nightingale

JOHN KEATS

My heart aches, and a drowsy numbness pains
  My sense, as though of hemlock I had drunk,
Or emptied some dull opiate to the drains
  One minute past, and Lethe-wards had sunk:
'Tis not through envy of thy happy lot,
  But being too happy in thy happiness –
    That thou, light-wingèd Dryad of the trees,
      In some melodious plot
  Of beechen green, and shadows numberless,
    Singest of summer in full-throated ease.

O, for a draught of vintage! that hath been
  Cooled a long age in the deep-delvèd earth,
Tasting of Flora and the country green,
  Dance, and Provençal song, and sunburnt mirth!
O for a beaker full of the warm South,
  Full of the true, the blushful Hippocrene,
    With beaded bubbles winking at the brim,
      And purple-stainèd mouth;
  That I might drink, and leave the world unseen,
    And with thee fade away into the forest dim:

Fade far away, dissolve, and quite forget
  What thou among the leaves hast never known,
The weariness, the fever, and the fret
  Here, where men sit and hear each other groan;
Where palsy shakes a few, sad, last grey hairs,
  Where youth grows pale, and spectre-thin, and dies;
    Where but to think is to be full of sorrow
      And leaden-eyed despairs;
    Where Beauty cannot keep her lustrous eyes,
      Or new Love pine at them beyond to-morrow.

Away! away! for I will fly to thee,
  Not charioted by Bacchus and his pards,
But on the viewless wings of Poesy,
  Though the dull brain perplexes and retards:
Already with thee! tender is the night,
  And haply the Queen-Moon is on her throne,
    Clustered around by all her starry Fays;
      But here there is no light,
  Save what from heaven is with the breezes blown
    Through verdurous glooms and winding mossy ways.

I cannot see what flowers are at my feet,
  Nor what soft incense hangs upon the boughs,
But, in embalmèd darkness, guess each sweet
  Wherewith the seasonable month endows
The grass, the thicket, and the fruit-tree wild;
  White hawthorn, and the pastoral eglantine;
    Fast-fading violets covered up in leaves;
      And mid-May's eldest child,
  The coming musk-rose, full of dewy wine,
    The murmurous haunt of flies on summer eves.

Darkling I listen; and for many a time
  I have been half in love with easeful Death,
Called him soft names in many a musèd rhyme,
  To take into the air my quiet breath;
Now more than ever seems it rich to die,
  To cease upon the midnight with no pain,
    While thou art pouring forth thy soul abroad
      In such an ecstasy!
  Still wouldst thou sing, and I have ears in vain –
    To thy high requiem become a sod.

Thou wast not born for death, immortal Bird!
   No hungry generations tread thee down;
The voice I hear this passing night was heard
   In ancient days by emperor and clown:
Perhaps the self-same song that found a path
    Through the sad heart of Ruth, when, sick for home,
      She stood in tears amid the alien corn;
        The same that oft-times hath
    Charmed magic casements, opening on the foam
      Of perilous seas, in faery lands forlorn.

Forlorn! the very word is like a bell
   To toll me back from thee to my sole self!
Adieu! the fancy cannot cheat so well
   And she is fam'd to do, deceiving elf.
Adieu! adieu! thy plaintive anthem fades
    Past the near meadows, over the still stream,
      Up the hill-side; and now 'tis buried deep
      In the next valley-glades:
    Was it a vision, or a waking dream?
    Fled is that music; Do I wake or sleep?

The Moon

ROBERT LOUIS STEVENSON

The moon has a face like the clock in the hall;
She shines on thieves on the garden wall,
On streets and fields and harbour quays,
And birdies asleep in the forks of the trees.

The squalling cat and the squeaking mouse,
The howling dog by the door of the house,
The bat that lies in bed at noon,
All love to be out by the light of the moon.

But all of the things that belong to the day
Cuddle to sleep to be out of her way;
And flowers and children close their eyes
Till up in the morning the sun shall arise.

Address to a Child during a Boisterous Winter Evening

DOROTHY WORDSWORTH

What way does the Wind come? What way does he go?
He rides over the water, and over the snow,
Through wood and through vale; and o'er rocky height
Which the goat cannot climb, takes his sounding flight;
 He tosses about in every bare tree,
 As, if you look up, you plainly may see;
But how he will come, and whither he goes,
There's never a scholar in England knows.

He will suddenly stop in a cunning nook,
And ring a sharp 'larum – but if you should look,
There's nothing to see but a cushion of snow
 Round as a pillow, and whiter than milk,
 And softer than if it were covered with silk.
Sometimes he'll hide in the cave of a rock,
Then whistle as shrill as the buzzard cock;
 Yet seek him – and what shall you find in the place?
 Nothing but silence and empty space;
Save, in a corner, a heap of dry leaves,
That he's left for a bed, to beggars or thieves.

As soon as 'tis daylight to-morrow, with me
You shall go to the orchard, and then you will see
That he has been there, and made a great rout,
And cracked the branches, and strewn them about;
 Heaven grant that he spare but that one upright twig
 That looked up at the sky so proud and big
All last summer, as well you know,
Studded with apples, a beautiful show!

Hark! over the roof he makes a pause,
And growls as if he would fix his claws

Right in the slates, and with a huge rattle
Drive them down, like men in a battle:
 But let him range round: he does us no harm,
 We build up the fire; we're snug and warm,
Untouched by his breath, see the candle shines bright,
And burns with a clear and steady light;
Books have we to read – but that half-stifled knell,
Alas, 'tis the sound of the eight o'clock bell.

Come now we'll to bed! And when we are there
He may work his own will, and what shall we care?
He may knock at the door – we'll not let him in;
May drive at the windows – we'll laugh at his din.
Let him seek his own home wherever it be;
Here's a cosy warm house for Edward and me.

Birthright

JOHN DRINKWATER

Lord Rameses of Egypt sighed
Because a summer evening passed;
And little Ariadne cried
That summer fancy fell at last
To dust; and young Verona died
When beauty's hour was overcast.

Theirs was the bitterness we know
Because the clouds of hawthorn keep
So short a state, and kisses go
To tombs unfathomably deep,
While Rameses and Romeo
And little Ariadne sleep.

The Red Fisherman: or The Devil's Decoy

WINTHROP MACKWORTH PRAED

The Abbot arose, and closed his book,
    And donned his sandal shoon,
And wandered forth, alone, to look
    Upon the summer moon:

The Abbot was weary as abbot could be,
And he sat down to rest on the stump of a tree:
When suddenly rose a dismal tone –
Was it a song, or was it a moan?
            'O ho! O ho!
            Above – below –
Lightly and brightly they glide and go!
The hungry and keen on the top are leaping,
The lazy and fat in the depths are sleeping;
Fishing is fine when the pool is muddy,
Broiling is rich when the coals are ruddy.'
In a monstrous fright, by the murky light,
He looked to the left and he looked to the right,
And what was the vision close before him,
That flung such a sudden stupor o'er him?
'Twas a sight to make the hair uprise,
    And the life blood colder run;
The startled priest struck both his thighs,
    And the abbey clock struck one!

All alone, by the side of the pool,
A tall man sat on a three-legged stool,
Kicking his heels on the dewy sod,
And putting in order his reel and rod;
Red were the rags his shoulders wore,
And a high red cap on his head he bore;

His arms and his legs were long and bare;
And two or three locks of long red hair
Were tossing about his scraggy neck,
Like a tattered flag o'er a splitting wreck.
It might be time, or it might be trouble,
Had bent that stout back nearly double.

The line the Abbot saw him throw
Had been fashioned and formed long ages ago,
And the hands that worked his foreign vest
Long ages ago had gone to their rest:
You would have sworn, as you looked on them,
He had finished in the flood with Ham and Shem!

There was turning of keys, and creaking of locks,
As he took forth a bait from his iron box.
Minnow or gentle, worm or fly –
It seemed not such to the Abbot's eye;
Gaily it glittered with jewel and gem,
And its shape was the shape of a diadem.
It was fastened a gleaming hook about
By a chain within and a chain without,
The fisherman gave it a kick and a spin,
And the water fizzed as it tumbled in!

From top to toe the Abbot shook,
As the fisherman armed his golden hook,
And awfully were his features wrought
By some dark dream or wakened thought.
Fixed as a monument, still as air,
He bent no knee, and he breathed no prayer;
But he signed – he knew not why or how –
The sign of the Cross on his clammy brow.

There was turning of keys and creaking of locks,
As he stalked away with his iron box.
   O ho! O ho!
    The cock doth crow;
It is time for the Fisher to rise and go.

8 · SWEET CONTENT

—

A Song of Good Heart

CONSTANCE HOLME

Give, dear O Lord,
　　Fine weather in its day,
Plenty on the board,
　　And a Good Heart all the way.

Kind soil for the share,
　　Kind sun for the ley,
Fair crop and to spare,
　　And a Good Heart all the way.

Good Hand with the stock,
　　Good Help and Hope aye,
Christ-blessing on the flock,
　　And a Good Heart all the way.

Gold-yellow on the corn,
　　Green-yellow on the hay,
A whistle in the morn,
　　And a Good Heart all the way.

Good Heart in the field,
　　And the Home-Heart gay.
Ay! Heaven yield
　　A Good Heart all the way!

A last prayer in the night
　　That God 'ild the day.
Bide still and die light,
　　With a Good Heart all the way.

A Boy's Song

JAMES HOGG

Where the pools are bright and deep,
Where the grey trout lies asleep,
Up the river and o'er the lea,
That's the way for Billy and me.

Where the blackbird sings the latest,
Where the hawthorn blooms the sweetest,
Where the nestlings chirp and flee,
That's the way for Billy and me.

Where the mowers mow the cleanest,
Where the hay lies thick and greenest;
There to trace the homeward bee,
That's the way for Billy and me.

Where the hazel bank is steepest,
Where the shadow falls the deepest,
Where the clustering nuts fall free,
That's the way for Billy and me.

Why the boys should drive away
Little sweet maidens from their play,
Or love the banter and fight so well,
That's the thing I never could tell.

But this I know, I love to play
Through the meadow, among the hay;
Up the water and o'er the lea,
That's the way for Billy and me.

Meg Merrilees

JOHN KEATS

Old Meg she was a Gipsy,
  And lived upon the moors:
Her bed it was the brown heath turf,
  And her house was out of doors.

Her apples were swart blackberries,
  Her currants pods o' broom;
Her wine was dew of the wild white rose,
  Her book a churchyard tomb.

Her Brothers were the craggy hills,
  Her Sisters larchen trees;
Alone with her great family
  She lived as she did please.

No breakfast had she many a morn,
  No dinner many a noon,
And 'stead of supper she would stare
  Full hard against the Moon.

But every morn of woodbine fresh
  She made her garlanding,
And every night the dark glen Yew
  She wove, and she would sing.

And with her fingers, old and brown,
  She plaited Mats o' Rushes,
And gave them to the Cottagers
  She met among the Bushes.

Old Meg was brave as Margaret Queen,
  And tall as Amazon;
An old red blanket cloak she wore;
  A chip hat had she on.
God rest her aged bones somewhere –
  She died full long agone!

Private Wealth

ROBERT HERRICK

Though Clock,
To tell how night drawes hence, I've none,
   A Cock
I have, to sing how day drawes on.
   I have
A maid (my Prew) by good luck sent,
   To save
That little, Fates me gave or lent.
   A Hen
I keep, which creaking day by day,
   Tells when
She goes her long white egg to lay.
   A Goose
I have, which, with a jealous care
   Lets loose
Her tongue, to tell what danger's neare.
   A Lamb
I keep (tame) with my morsells fed,
   Whose Dam
An Orphan left him (lately dead).
   A Cat
I keep, that playes about my House,
   Grown fat,
With eating many a miching Mouse.
   To these
A Trasy* I do keep, whereby
   I please
The more my rurall privacie:

* His spaniel

237

Which are
But toyes, to give my heart some ease:
Where care
None is, slight things do lightly please.

Part of an Ode

BEN JONSON

It is not growing like a tree
In bulk, doth make men better be;
Or standing long – an oak, three hundred year –
   To fall at last, dry, bald and sere.
      A lily of a day
      Is fairer far in May.
Although it fall and die that night
It was the plant and flower of light.
   In small proportions we just beauties see,
   And in short measures, life may perfect be.

Sweet Content

THOMAS DEKKER

Art thou poor, yet hast thou golden slumbers?
  O sweet content?
Art thou rich, yet is thy mind perplexed?
  O punishment!
Dost thou laugh to see how fools are vexed
To add to golden numbers, golden numbers?
O sweet content! O sweet, O sweet content!

 Work apace, apace, apace;
 Honest labour bears a lovely face;
 Then hey nonny nonny, hey nonny, nonny!

Canst drink the waters of the crispèd spring?
  O sweet content!
Swimm'st thou in wealth, yet sink'st in thine own tears?
  O punishment!
Then he that patiently want's burden bears,
No burden bears, but is a king, a king!
O sweet content! O sweet, O sweet content!

 Work apace, apace, apace;
 Honest labour bears a lovely face;
 Then hey nonny nonny, hey nonny, nonny!

A Wish

SAMUEL ROGERS

Mine be a cot beside the hill;
   A bee-hive's hum shall soothe my ear,
A willowy brook that turns a mill
   With many a fall, shall linger near.

The swallow oft beneath my thatch
   Shall twitter from her clay-built nest;
Oft shall the pilgrim lift the latch
   And share my meal, a welcome guest.

Around my ivied porch shall spring
   Each fragrant flower that drinks the dew,
And Lucy at her wheel shall sing,
   In russet gown and apron blue.

On his Blindness

JOHN MILTON

When I consider how my light is spent,
  Ere half my days, in this dark world and wide,
  And that one Talent which is death to hide,
Lodged with me useless, though my Soul more bent
To serve therewith my Maker, and present
  My true account, lest He returning chide;
  'Doth God exact day-labour, light denied?'
I fondly ask: but Patience, to prevent
That murmur, soon replies 'God doth not need
  Either man's work, or his own gifts: who best
    Bear his mild yoke, they serve him best; his State
Is Kingly. Thousands at his bidding speed,
  And post o'er land and ocean without rest;
    They also serve who only stand and wait.'

The Grasshopper and Cricket

JOHN KEATS

The poetry of earth is never dead:
  When all the birds are faint with the hot sun,
  And hide in cooling trees, a voice will run
From hedge to hedge about the new-mown mead;
That is the Grasshopper's – he takes the lead
  In summer luxury – he has never done
  With his delights; for when tired out with fun
He rests at ease beneath some pleasant weed.
The poetry of earth is ceasing never:
  On a lone winter evening, when the frost
    Has wrought a silence, from the stove there shrills
The Cricket's song, in warmth increasing ever,
  And seems to one in drowsiness half lost,
    The Grasshopper's among some grassy hills.

Minchmoor

HAMILTON OF BANGOUR

Sweet smells the birk: green grows, green grows the grass,
  Yellow on Yarrow's banks the gowan.
Fair hangs the apple frae the rock,
  Sweet the wave of Yarrow flowan.

Flows Yarrow sweet? As sweet, as sweet flows Tweed!
  As green its grass, its gowan yellow;
As sweet smells, on its braes, the birk;
  The apple frae the rock as mellow.

Clear had the Day been

MICHAEL DRAYTON

Clear had the day been from the dawn,
  All chequered was the sky,
Thin clouds, like scarves of cobweb lawn,
  Veiled heaven's most glorious eye.

The wind had no more strength than this,
  – That leisurely it blew –
To make one leaf the next to kiss
  That closely by it grew.

The rills, that on the pebbles played,
  Might now be heard at will;
This world the only music made,
  Else everything was still.

Fear no More

WILLIAM SHAKESPEARE

Fear no more the heat o' the sun,
Nor the furious winter's rages,
Thou thy worldly task hast done,
Home art gone, and ta'en thy wages.
  Golden lads and girls all must,
  As chimney-sweepers, come to dust.

Fear no more the frown o' the great,
Thou art past the tyrant's stroke;
Care no more to clothe, and eat,
To thee the reed is as the oak;
  The sceptre, learning, physick must,
  All follow this and come to dust.

Fear no more the lightning flash,
Nor the all-dreaded thunder-stone,
Fear not slander, censure rash,
Thou hast finished joy and moan.
    All lovers young, all lovers must,
    Consign to thee, and come to dust.

Song

CHRISTINA ROSSETTI

When I am dead, my dearest,
    Sing no sad songs for me;
Plant thou no roses at my head,
    Nor shady cypress tree:
Be the green grass above me
    With showers and dewdrops wet;
And if thou wilt, remember,
    And if thou wilt, forget.

I shall not see the shadows,
    I shall not feel the rain;
I shall not hear the nightingale
    Sing on as if in pain:
And dreaming through the twilight
    That doth not rise nor set,
Haply I may remember,
    And haply may forget.

To One who has been Long in City Pent

JOHN KEATS

To one who has been long in city pent,
　'Tis very sweet to look into the fair
　And open face of heaven – to breathe a prayer
Full in the smile of the blue firmament.
Who is more happy, when, with hearts content,
　Fatigued he sinks into some pleasant lair
　Of wavy grass, and reads a debonair
And gentle tale of love and languishment?
Returning home at evening, with an ear
　Catching the notes of Philomel – an eye
Watching the sailing cloudlet's bright career,
　He mourns that day so soon has glided by:
E'en like the passage of an angel's tear
　That falls through the clear ether silently.

Jerusalem

WILLIAM BLAKE

And did those feet in ancient time
Walk upon England's mountains green?
And was the Holy Lamb of God
On England's pleasant pastures seen?

And did the countenance divine
Shine forth upon our clouded hills?
And was Jerusalem builded here
Among these dark satanic mills?

Bring me my bow of burning gold!
Bring me my arrows of desire!
Bring me my spear! O clouds, unfold!
Bring me my chariot of fire!

I will not cease from mental fight,
Nor shall my sword sleep in my hand,
Till we have built Jerusalem
In England's green and pleasant land.

Ode on Intimations of Immortality

WILLIAM WORDSWORTH

There was a time when meadow, grove, and stream,
The earth, and every common sight,
    To me did seem
   Apparelled in celestial light,
The glory and the freshness of a dream.
It is now as it hath been of yore;
  Turn wheresoe'er I may,
    By night or day,
The things which I have seen I now can see no more.

    The Rainbow comes and goes,
    And lovely is the Rose,
    The Moon doth with delight
Look round her when the heavens are bare,
    Waters on a starry night
    Are beautiful and fair;
  The sunshine is a glorious birth;
  But yet I know, where'er I go,
That there hath past away a glory from the earth.

Now, while the birds thus sing a joyous song,
  And while the young lambs bound
   As to the tabor's sound,
To me alone there came a thought of grief:
A timely utterance gave that thought relief,
    And I again am strong:
The cataracts blow their trumpets from the steep;
No more shall grief of mine the season wrong:
I hear the Echoes through the mountains throng,
The Winds come to me from the fields of sleep,

And all the earth is gay.
    Land and sea
Give themselves up to jollity,
    And with the heart of May
Doth every Beast keep holiday.
    Thou Child of Joy,
Shout round me, let me hear thy shouts, thou happy shepherd-boy!

Upon Westminster Bridge

SEPTEMBER 3RD, 1802

WILLIAM WORDSWORTH

Earth has not anything to show more fair;
    Dull would he be of soul who could pass by
    A sight so touching in its majesty;
This City now doth, like a garment, wear
The beauty of the morning; silent, bare,
    Ships, towers, domes, theatres, and temples lie
    Open unto the fields, and to the sky;
All bright and glittering in the smokeless air.
Never did sun more beautifully steep
    In his first splendour, valley, rock, or hill;
Ne'er saw I, never felt, a calm so deep!
    The river glideth at his own sweet will:
Dear God! the very houses seem asleep:
    And all that mighty heart is lying still!

9 · CHRISTMAS

—

Now Thrice Welcome Christmas

ANONYMOUS

Now thrice welcome, Christmas,
  Which brings us good cheer,
Minc'd pies and plum porridge,
  Good ale and strong beer;
With pig, goose, and capon,
  The best that can be,
So well doth the weather
  And our stomachs agree.

Observe how the chimneys
  Do smoke all about,
The cooks are providing
  For dinner, no doubt;
For those on whose tables
  No victuals appear,
O may they keep Lent
  All the rest of the year!

With holly and ivy
  So green and so gay,
We deck up our houses
  As fresh as the day,
With bays and rosemary,
  And laurel complete;
And every one now
  Is a king in conceit.

Christmas Carol

ELEANOR FARJEON

God bless your house this Holy night,
   And all within it:

God bless the candle that you light,
   To midnight's minute;

The board at which you break your bread,
   The cup you drink of:

And as you raise it, the unsaid
   Name that you think of:

The warming fire, the bed of rest,
   The ringing laughter:

These things and all things else be blest
   From floor to rafter

This Holy night, from dark to light,
   Even more than other:

And if you have no house to-night,
   God bless you, brother.

Adam lay Ybounden

FIFTEENTH-CENTURY CAROL

ANONYMOUS

Adam lay ybounden,
  Bounden in a bond;
Four thousand winter
  Thought he not too long.
And all was for an apple,
  An apple that he took,
As clerkës finden
  Written in their book.
Nor had the apple taken been,
  The apple taken been,
Then had never our Lady
  A-been heaven's queen.
Blessed be the time
  That apple taken was!
Therefore we may singen
  Deo gracias!

As Dew in April

FIFTEENTH-CENTURY CAROL

ANONYMOUS

I sing of a maiden
 That is makeles;
King of all kings
 To her Son she ches.

He came all so still
 There His mother was,
As dew in April
 That falleth on the grass.

He came all so still
 To His mother's bower,
As dew in April
 That falleth on the flower.

He came all so still
 There His mother lay,
As dew in April
 That falleth on the spray.

Mother and maiden
 Was never none but she;
Well may such a lady
 Godés mother be.

A Christmas Carol

CHRISTINA ROSSETTI

In the bleak mid-winter
  Frosty wind made moan,
Earth stood hard as iron,
  Water like a stone;
Snow had fallen, snow on snow,
  Snow on snow,
In the bleak mid-winter
  Long ago.

Our God, heaven cannot hold Him,
  Nor earth sustain;
Heaven and earth shall flee away
  When He comes to reign:
In the bleak mid-winter
  A stable-place sufficed
The Lord God Almighty,
  Jesus Christ.

What can I give Him,
  Poor as I am?
If I were a shepherd
  I would bring a lamb;
If I were a wise man
  I would do my part –
Yet what I can, I give Him,
  Give my heart.

Saint Stephen was a Clerk

FIFTEENTH-CENTURY CAROL

ANONYMOUS

Saint Stephen was a clerk in King Herod's hall,
And served him of bread and cloth, as ever King befall.

Stephen out of kitchen came with boar's head in hand,
He saw a star was fair and bright over Bethlehem stand.

He cast adown the boar's head and went into the hall:
'I forsake thee, King Herod, and thy workés all,

'I forsake thee, King Herod, and thy workés all;
There is a child in Bethlehem born is better than we all.'

'What aileth thee, Stephen, what is thee befall?
Lacketh thee either meat or drink in King Herod's hall?'

'Lacketh me neither meat nor drink in King Herod's hall,
There is a child in Bethlehem born is better than we all.'

'What aileth thee, Stephen, art thou mad, or ginnest thou to brede?
Lacketh thee either gold or fee or any riché weed?'

'Lacketh me neither gold nor fee, nor no riché weed,
There is a child in Bethlehem born shall help us at our need.'

'That is all so sooth, Stephen, all so sooth ywis,
As this capon crow shall that lieth here in my dish.'

That word was not so sooné said, that word in that hall,
The capon crew, *Christus Natus est,* among the lordés all.

'Riseth up my tormentors, by twos and all by one,
And leadeth Stephen out of this town, and stoneth him with stone.'

Took they then Stephen and stoned him in the way,
Therefore is his even on Christés own day.

The Wassail

ROBERT HERRICK

Give way, give way, ye gates, and win
   An easy blessing to your bin
And basket by our entering in.

May both with manchet stand replete;
   Your larders too so hung with meat
That, though a thousand thousand eat,

Yet, ere twelve moons shall whirl about
   Their silvery spheres, there's none may doubt
But more's sent in than was serv'd out.

Next may your dairies prosper so
   As that your pans no ebb may know;
But if they do, the more to flow,

Like to a solemn sober stream,
   Banked all with lilies and the cream
Of sweetest cowslips filling them.

Then may your plants be pressed with fruit,
   Nor bee or hive you have be mute,
But sweetly sounding like a lute.

Next may your duck and teaming hen
   Both to the cock's tread say Amen,
And for their two eggs render ten.

Last may your harrows, shares, and ploughs,
   Your stacks, your stocks, your sweetest mows,
All prosper by your virgin vows.

Alas! we bless, but see none here
   That brings us either ale or beer;
In a dry house all things are near.

Let's leave a longer time to wait,
   When rust and cobwebs bind the gate
And all live here with needy Fate.

Where chimneys do forever weep
   For want of warmth, and stomachs keep
With noise the servants' eyes from sleep.

It is in vain to sing or stay
   Our free feet here; but we'll away:
Yet to the Lares this we'll say –

The time will come when you'll be sad
   And reckon this for fortune bad,
T'have lost the good ye might have had.

The Holly and the Ivy

FIFTEENTH-CENTURY CAROL

ANONYMOUS

Holly stands in the hall, fair to behold,
Ivy stands without the door, she is full sore a-cold.
   Nay, ivy, nay, it shall not be y-wis,
   Let holly have the mastery as the manner is.

Holly and his merry men they dancen and they sing,
Ivy and her maidens they weepen and they wring:
   Nay, ivy, nay, it shall not be y-wis,
   Let holly have the mastery as the manner is.

Ivy hath a kibe, she caught it with the cold;
So may they all have one, that with ivy hold.
   Nay, ivy, nay, it shall not be y-wis,
   Let holly have the mastery as the manner is.

Holly hath berries as red as any rose,
The forester, the hunters keep them fro the does.
   Nay, ivy, nay, it shall not be y-wis,
   Let holly have the mastery as the manner is.

Ivy hath berries as black as any sloes,
Then comes the owl and eats them as she goes.
   Nay, ivy, nay, it shall not be y-wis,
   Let holly have the mastery as the manner is.

Holly hath birdés a full fair flock,
The nightingale, the popinjay, and the gentle laverock.
   Nay, ivy, nay, it shall not be y-wis,
   Let holly have the mastery as the manner is.

Good ivy, what birdés hast thou?
None but the owlet that cries 'How, how!'
   Nay, ivy, nay, it shall not be y-wis,
   Let holly have the mastery as the manner is.

The Cherry-Tree Carol

ANONYMOUS

As Joseph was a-walking
  He heard an angel sing:
'This night shall be born
  Our heavenly king;

'He neither shall be born
  In housen or in hall,
Nor in the place of Paradise,
  But in an ox's stall.

'He neither shall be clothed
  In purple or in pall,
But all in fair linen,
  As were babies all.

'He neither shall be rocked
  In silver or in gold,
But in a wooden cradle
  That rocks on the mould.

'He neither shall be christened
  In white wine or red,
But with fair spring water
  With which we were christenéd.'

*   *   *

— Mary took her young son
  And set him on her knee;
'I pray thee now, Dear Child,
  Tell me how this world shall be.'

'O I shall be as dead, mother,
  As the stones in the wall:
O the stones in the streets, mother,
  Shall mourn for me all.

'And upon a Wednesday
  My vow I will make,
And upon Good Friday
  My death I will take.

'Upon Easter-day, mother,
  My up-rising shall be:
O the sun and the moon, mother,
  Shall both rise with me.

'The people shall rejoice,
  And the birds they shall sing,
To see the uprising
  Of the heavenly king.'

Christmas Bells

HENRY WADSWORTH LONGFELLOW

I heard the bells on Christmas Day
Their old familiar carols play,
   And wild and sweet
   The words repeat
Of Peace on earth, Good-will to men!

And thought how, as the day had come,
The belfries of all Christendom
   Had rolled along
   The unbroken song
Of Peace on earth, Good-will to men!

Till ringing, singing on its way,
The world revolved from night to day,
   A voice, a chime,
   A chant sublime,
Of Peace on earth, Good-will to men!

Then from each black accursed mouth,
The cannon thundered in the South,
   And with the sound
   The carols drowned,
The Peace on earth, Good-will to men!

And in despair I bowed my head;
'There is no peace on earth,' I said,
   'For hate is strong
   And mocks the song
Of Peace on earth, Good-will to men!'

Then peeled the bells more loud and deep:
'God is not dead, nor doth he sleep!
    The Wrong shall fail,
    The Right prevail,
With Peace on earth, Good-will to men!'

10 · PRAISE AND THANKSGIVING

—

Prayer at Bedtime

ANONYMOUS

Matthew, Mark, Luke, and John
Bless the bed that I lie on.
Before I lay me down to sleep,
I pray the Lord my soul to keep.

Four corners to my bed,
Four angels there are spread;
Two at the foot, two at the head:
Four to carry me when I'm dead.

I go by sea, I go by land:
The Lord made me with His right hand.
Should any danger come to me,
Sweet Jesus Christ deliver me.

He's the branch and I'm the flower,
Pray God send me a happy hour;
And should I die before I wake,
I pray the Lord my soul to take.

A Ternarie of Littles, upon a Pipkin of Jelly sent to a Lady

ROBERT HERRICK

A little Saint best fits a little Shrine,
A little Prop best fits a little Vine,
As my small Cruse best fits my little Wine.

A little Seed best fits a little Soil,
A little Trade best fits a little Toil:
As my small Jar best fits my little Oil.

A little Bin best fits a little Bread,
A little Garland fits a little Head:
As my small Stuff best fits my little Shed.

A little Hearth best fits a little Fire,
A little Chapel fits a little Choir,
As my small Bell best fits my little Spire.

A little Stream best fits a little Boat,
A little Lead best fits a little Float,
As my small Pipe best fits my little Note.

A little Meat best fits a little Belly,
As sweetly, Lady, give me leave to tell'ee,
This little Pipkin fits this little Jelly.

Home Thoughts from the Sea

ROBERT BROWNING

Nobly, nobly Cape Saint Vincent
    to the North-West died away;
Sunset ran, one glorious blood-red,
    reeking into Cadiz Bay;
Bluish 'mid the burning water,
    full in face Trafalgar lay;
In the dimmest North-East distance
    dawned Gibraltar, grand and grey;

'Here and here did England help me:
    How can I help England?' – say,
Whoso turns as I, this evening,
    turn to God to praise and pray,
While Jove's planet rises yonder,
    silent over Africa.

His Alms

ROBERT HERRICK

Here, here I live,
And somewhat give,
Of what I have,
To those, who crave.
Little or much,
My alms is such:
But if my deal
Of oil and meal
Shall fuller grow,
More I'll bestow:
Meantime be it
E'en but a bit,
Or else a crumb,
The scrip hath some.

Psalm 23

AUTHORIZED VERSION

The Lord is my shepherd;
I shall not want.
He maketh me to lie down in green pastures;
He leadeth me beside the still waters.
He restoreth my soul:
He leadeth me in the paths of righteousness
For his name's sake.

Yea, though I walk through the valley of the shadow of death,
I will fear no evil:
For thou art with me;
Thy rod and thy staff, they comfort me.

Thou preparest a table before me
In the presence of mine enemies;
Thou anointest my head with oil;
My cup runneth over.

Surely goodness and mercy shall follow me
All the days of my life:
And I will dwell in the house of the Lord
For ever.

Psalm 127

VERSES I AND 2

AUTHORIZED VERSION

Except the Lord build the house,
They labour in vain that build it:
Except the Lord keep the city,
The watchman waketh but in vain.

It is vain for you to rise up early,
To sit up late,
To eat the bread of sorrows:
For so he giveth his beloved sleep.

Psalm 126

AUTHORIZED VERSION

When the Lord turned again the captivity of Zion,
We were like them that dream.
Then was our mouth filled with laughter,
And our tongue with singing:
Then said they among the heathen,
The Lord hath done great things for them.

The Lord hath done great things for us;
Whereof we are glad.
Turn again our captivity, O Lord,
As the streams in the South.

They that sow in tears
Shall reap in joy.
He that goeth forth and weepeth,
Bearing precious seed,
Shall doubtless come again with rejoicing,
Bringing his sheaves with him.

Psalm 137

VERSES 1–6

AUTHORIZED VERSION

By the rivers of Babylon, there we sat down,
Yea, we wept, when we remembered Zion.
We hanged our harps upon the willows
In the midst thereof.

For there they that carried us away captive
Required of us a song:
And they that wasted us, required of us mirth,
Saying: Sing us one of the songs of Zion.

How shall we sing the Lord's song
In a strange land?
If I forget thee, O Jerusalem,
Let my right hand forget her cunning.

If I do not remember thee,
Let my tongue cleave to the roof of my mouth:
If I prefer not Jerusalem
Above my chief joy.

His Creed

ROBERT HERRICK

I do believe that die I must
And be returned from out my dust:
I do believe that, when I rise,
Christ I shall see with these same eyes:
I do believe that I must come,
With others, to the dreadful doom:
I do believe the bad must go
From thence, to everlasting woe.
I do believe the good and I
Shall live with Him eternally:
I do believe I shall inherit
Heaven by Christ's mercies – not my merit:
I do believe the One in Three
And Three in perfect unity:
Lastly that Jesus is a deed
Of gift from God: And here's my Creed.

Salute to the Whole World

WALT WHITMAN

You, whoever you are!
You, daughter or son of England!
You of the mighty Slavic tribes and empires!
    You Russ in Russia!
You dim-descended, black, divine-souled African, large, fine-headed,
    Nobly-formed, superbly destined, on equal terms with me!

You Norwegian, Swede, Dane, Icelander! You Prussian!
You Spaniard of Spain, you Portuguese!
You Frenchwoman and Frenchman of France!
You Belge! you liberty-lover of the Netherlands!
You sturdy Austrian! You Lombard, Hun, Bohemian! farmer of
    Styria!
You neighbour of the Danube!
You working-man of the Rhine, the Elbe, or the Weser!
    You working-woman too!
You Sardinian! You Bavarian, Swabian, Saxon, Wallachian,
    Bulgarian!
You citizen of Prague! Roman, Neapolitan, Greek!
You lithe matador in the arena at Seville!
You mountaineer living lawlessly on the Taurus or Caucasus!
You Bokh horse-herd, watching your mares and stallions feeding!
You beautiful-bodied Persian, at full speed in the saddle, shooting
    arrows to the mark!
You Chinaman and Chinawoman of China! You Tartar of Tartary!
You women of the earth subordinated at your tasks!
You Jew journeying in your old age through every risk,
    To stand once more on Syrian ground!
You other Jews waiting in all lands for your Messiah!
You thoughtful Armenian, pondering by some stream of the
    Euphrates!

You peering amid the ruins of Nineveh! You ascending Mount
    Ararat!
You foot-worn pilgrim welcoming the far-away sparkle of the
    minarets of Meccah!

You sheiks along the stretch from Suez to Bab-el-mandeb, ruling
    your families and tribes!
You olive-grower tending your fruit on fields of Nazareth, Damas-
    cus, or Lake Tiberias!
You Thibet trader on the wide inland, or bargaining in the shops of
    Lassa!
You Japanese man or woman! you liver in Madagascar, Ceylon,
    Sumatra, Borneo!
All you continentals of Asia, Africa, Europe, Australia, indifferent of
    place!
All you on the numberless islands of the archipelagoes of the sea!
And you of centuries hence, when you listen to me!
And you, each and everywhere, whom I specify not, but include just
    the same!
Health to you!
Good will to you all – from me and America sent.
   Each of us inevitable;
Each of us limitless – each of us with his or her right upon the earth;
Each of us allowed the eternal purports of the earth;
Each of us here as divinely as any is here.

O, Lift one Thought

SAMUEL TAYLOR COLERIDGE

Stop, Christian passer-by! Stop, child of God,
And read with gentle breast. Beneath this sod
A poet lies, or that which once seemed he.
O, lift one thought in prayer for S.T.C.;
That he who many a year with toil of breath
Found death in life, may here find life in death.
Mercy for praise – to be forgiven for fame
He asked, and hoped, through Christ. Do thou the same!

Index of Authors

Index of First Lines

*If you have enjoyed reading this book and would
like to know about others which we publish, why
not join the Puffin Club? You will be sent the club
magazine,* Puffin Post, *four times a year and a
smart badge and membership book. You will also be
able to enter all the competitions. You will find an
application form on the next page.*

APPLICATION FOR MEMBERSHIP OF
THE PUFFIN CLUB

TO: THE PUFFIN CLUB SECRETARY,
PENGUIN BOOKS LTD,
HARMONDSWORTH, MIDDLESEX

Please enrol me in the Puffin Club. I enclose my
subscription for (please tick appropriate box)

Three Year Membership (£1)* ☐

One Year Membership (10s.)* ☐

Family Membership, 10s. a year plus 2s. 6d. for each
extra member.* ☐

Overseas Membership
School Membership } Please apply for further details.

(Write clearly in block letters)

Christian name(s)   Surname

Full Address (use a separate box for each line)

Boy or Girl............................... Date of Birth...............................

Signature ....

* Subject to alteration without prior notice.